MOTH

"A MIND AND A TALENT
OF UNCOMMON DIMENSIONS"
Harlan Ellison

"COMPELLING . . .
Sallis is a rare find for mystery readers,
a fine prose stylist with an interest
in moral struggle and a gift for the
lacerating evocation of loss."
New York Newsday

"EVEN STRONGER THAN
THE LONG-LEGGED FLY . . .
A walk on Louisiana's wild side."
Kirkus Reviews

"SALLIS IS A MASTERFUL WRITER
vigorously exploring the seemingly inexhaustible
territory of the post–modern detective novel."
New Orleans Times-Picayune

"OFFERS PLENTIFUL SATISFACTION . . .
Rich characterization, captivating rhythms
and lyrical voice"
Publishers Weekly

"AN OUTSTANDING NOVEL . . .
Sallis' writing hovers just at the edge of brilliance."
Booklist

Other Avon Books by
James Sallis

THE LONG-LEGGED FLY

MOTH

James Sallis

AVON BOOKS  NEW YORK

AVON BOOKS
A division of
The Hearst Corporation
1350 Avenue of the Americas
New York, New York 10019

Copyright © 1993 by James Sallis
Inside cover author photo by David Spielman
Published by arrangement with Carroll & Graf Publishers, Inc.
Library of Congress Catalog Card Number: 93-24739
ISBN: 0-380-72377-8

First Avon Books Printing: August 1995

AVON TRADEMARK REG. U.S. PAT. OFF. AND IN OTHER COUNTRIES, MARCA REGISTRADA, HECHO EN U.S.A.

Printed in the U.S.A.

RA   10 9 8 7 6 5 4 3 2 1

To the memory of
Chester Himes

Father, the dark moths
Crouch at the sills of the earth, waiting.

—JAMES WRIGHT

MOTH

IT WAS MIDNIGHT, IT WAS RAINING.

I scrubbed at the sink as instructed, and went on in. The second set of double doors led into a corridor at the end of which, to the left, a woman sat at a U-shaped desk behind an improvised levee of computers, phones, stacks of paperwork and racks of bound files. She was on the phone, trying simultaneously to talk into it and respond to the youngish man in soiled Nikes and lab coat who stood beside her asking about results of lab tests. Every few moments the phone purred and a new light started blinking on it. The woman herself was not young, forty to fifty, with thinning hair in a teased style out of fashion for at least twenty years. A tag on her yellow polyester jacket read Jo Ellen Heslip. Names are important.

To the right I walked past closetlike rooms filled with steel racks of supplies, an X-ray viewer, satellite pharmacy, long conference tables. Then into the intensive-care nursery, the NICU, itself—like coming out onto a plain. It was half the size of a football field, broken into semidiscrete sections by four-foot tile walls topped with open shelving. (Pods, I'd later learn to call them.) Light flooded in from windows along three walls. The windows were double, sealed: thick outer glass, an enclosed area in which lint and construction debris had settled, inner pane. Pigeons strutted on the sill outside. Down in the street buses slowed at, then passed, a covered stop. Someone in

1

a hospital gown, impossible to say what sex or age, slept therein on a bench advertising Doctor's Bookstore, getting up from time to time to rummage in the trash barrel alongside, pulling out cans with a swallow or two remaining, a bag of Zapp's chips, a smashed carton from Popeye's.

I found Pod 1 by trial and error and made my way through the grid of incubators, open cribs, radiant warmers: terms I'd come to know in weeks ahead. Looking down at pink and blue tags affixed to these containers.

Baby Girl McTell lay in an incubator in a corner beneath the window. The respirator reared up beside her on its pole like a silver sentinel, whispering: *shhhh, shhhh, shhhh.* LED displays wavered and changed on its face. With each *shhhh,* Baby Girl McTell's tiny body puffed up, and a rack of screens mounted above her to the right also updated: readouts of heart rate, respiration and various internal pressures on a Hewlett-Packard monitor, oxygen saturation on a Nellcor pulse oximeter, levels of CO_2 and O_2 from transcutaneous monitors.

> Baby Girl McTell
> Born 9/15
> Weight 1 lb 5 oz
> Mother Alouette

I could hold her in the palm of my hand, easily, I thought. Or could have, if not for this battleship of machinery keeping her afloat, keeping her alive.

The nurse at bedside looked up. Papers lay scattered about on the bedside stand. She was copying from them onto another, larger sheet. She was left-handed, her wrist a winglike curve above the pen.

"Good morning. Would you be the father, by any chance?"

Reddish-blond hair cut short. Wearing scrubs, as they

all were. Bright green eyes and a British accent like clear, pure water, sending a stab of pain and longing and loss through me as I thought of Vicky: red hair floating above me when I woke with DT's in Touro Infirmary, Vicky with her Scottish *r*'s, Vicky who had helped me retrieve my life and then gone away.

Teresa Hunt, according to her nametag. But did I really look like an eighteen-year-old's romantic other?

Or maybe she meant the *girl's* father?

I shook my head. "A family friend."

"Well, I had wondered." Words at a level, unaccented. "No one's seen anything of him, as far as I know."

"From what little *I* know, I don't expect you will."

"I see. Well, we are rather accustomed to that, I suppose. Some of the mothers themselves stop coming after a time."

She shuffled papers together and capped her pen, which hung on a cord around her neck. There was print on the side of it: advertising of some sort, drugs probably. Like the notepad Vicky wrote her name and phone number on when I found her at Hotel Dieu.

Tucking everything beneath an oversized clipboard, Teresa Hunt squared it on the stand.

"Look, I'm terribly sorry," she said. "Someone should have explained this to you, but only parents and grandparents are allowed—oh, never mind all that. Bugger the rules. What difference can it possibly make? Is this your first time to see her?"

I nodded.

"And it's the mother you know?"

"Grandmother, really. The baby's mother's mother. We . . . were friends. For a long time."

"I see." She probably did. "And the girl's mother recently died, according to the chart. A stroke, wasn't it?"

"It was."

There was no way I could tell her or anyone else what

LaVerne had meant, had been, to me. We were both little more than kids when we met; Verne was a hooker then. Years later she married her doctor and I didn't see her for a while. When he cut her loose, she started as a volunteer at a rape-crisis center and went on to a psychology degree and full-time counseling. It was a lonely life, I guess, at both ends. And when finally she met a guy named Chip Landrieu and married him, even as I began to realize what I had lost, I was happy for her. For both of them.

"Did she know Alouette was pregnant?"

I shook my head. "Their lives had gone separate ways many years back." So separate that I hadn't even known about Alouette. "She—" Say it, Lew. Go ahead and say her name. Names are important. "LaVerne had been trying to get back in touch, to find Alouette."

She looked away for a moment. "What's happened to us?" And in my own head I heard Vicky again, many years ago: What's wrong with this country, Lew? "Well, never mind all that. Not much we can do about it, is there? Do you understand what's happening here?" Her nod took in the ventilator, monitors, bags of IV medication hanging upside down like transparent bats from silver poles, Baby Girl McTell's impossible ark; perhaps the whole world.

"Not really." Does anyone, I wanted to add.

"Alouette is an habitual drug user. Crack, mainly, according to our H&P and the social worker's notes, but there's a history of drug and alcohol abuse involving many controlled substances, more or less whatever was available, it seems. She makes no attempt to deny this. And because of it, Alouette's baby was profoundly compromised *in utero*. She never developed, and though Alouette did manage to carry her as far as the seventh month, what you're looking at here in the incubator is something more on the order of a five-month embryo. You can see there's almost nothing to her. The eyes are fused, her skin breaks down wherever it's touched, there aren't any lungs to speak of. She's receiving medication which paralyzes her own respiratory efforts, and the machine, the ventilator, does all her breathing. We have her on high pressures and a high rate, and nine hours out of ten we're having to give her hundred-percent oxygen. *Two* hours out of ten, maybe, we're holding our own.''

''You're telling me she's going to die.''

''I am. Though of course I'm not supposed to.''

''Then why are we doing all this?''

''Because we can. Because we know how. There are sixty available beds in this unit. On any given day, six to ten of those beds will be filled with crack babies like Alouette's. At least ten others are just as sick, for whatever reasons—other kinds of drug and alcohol abuse, congenital disease, poor nutrition, lack of prenatal care. The numbers are climbing every day. When I first came here, there'd be, oh, five to ten babies in this unit. Now there're never fewer than thirty. And there've been times we've had to stack cribs in the hallway out there.''

''Are you always this blunt?''

''No. No, I'm not, not really. But we look on all this a bit differently in Britain, you understand. And I think that I may be answering something I see in your face, as well.''

''Thank you.'' I held out a hand. She took it without hesitation or deference, as American women seldom can. ''My name is Griffin. Lew.''

''Teresa, as you can see. And since Hunt is the name on my nursing license, I use it here. But in real life, *away* from here, I mostly use my maiden name, McKinney. If there's ever anything I can do, Mr. Griffin, please let me know. This can be terribly hard on a person.''

She removed vials from a drawer beneath the incubator, checked them against her lists, drew up portions into three separate syringes and injected these one at a time, and slowly, into crooks (called heplocks) in Baby Girl McTell's IV tubing. There were four IV sites, swaddled in tape. Almost every day one or another of them had to be restarted elsewhere, in her scalp, behind an ankle, wherever they could find a vein that wouldn't blow.

She dropped the syringes into the mouth of a red plastic Sharps container, pulled a sheet of paper from beneath the clipboard and, glancing at a clock on the wall nearby, made several notations.

"I don't know at all why I'm telling you this, Mr. Griffin, but I had a child myself, a son. He was three months early, weighed almost two pounds and lived just over eight days. I was sixteen at the time. And afterwards, because of an infection, I became quite sterile. But it was because of him that I first began thinking about becoming a nurse."

"Call me Lew. Please."

"I don't think the head nurse would care much for that, if she were to hear about it. She's a bit stuffy and proper, you understand."

"But what can one more rule matter? Since, as you say, we've already started breaking them."

"Yes, well, we have done that truly, haven't we, Lew. Do you think you'd be wanting to speak with one of the doctors? They should be along in just a bit. Or I could try paging one of them."

"Is there anything they can tell me that you can't?"

"Not really, no."

"Then I don't see any reason for bothering them. I'm sure they have plenty to do."

"That they have. Well, I'll just step out for a few minutes and leave the two of you to get acquainted. If you should need anything, Debbie will be watching over my children while I'm gone."

She nodded toward a nurse who sat in a rocking chair across the pod, bottle-feeding one of the babies.

"That's Andrew. He's been with us almost a year now, and we all spoil him just awfully, I'm afraid."

"A year? When will he leave?"

"There's nowhere for him to go. Most of his bowel

had to be removed just after birth, and he'll always be needing a lot of care. Feedings every hour, a colostomy to manage. His parents came to see him when the mother was in the hospital, but once she was discharged, we stopped hearing from them. The police went out to the address we had for them after a bit, but they were long gone. Eventually I suppose he'll be moved upstairs to pediatrics. And somewhere farther along they'll find a nursing home that will take him, perhaps.''

I looked from Andrew back to Baby Girl McTell as Teresa walked away. Names are important. Things are what we call them. By naming, we understand. But what name do we have for a baby who's never quite made it into life, who goes on clawing after it, all the while slipping further away, with a focus, a hunger, we can scarcely imagine? What can we call the battles going on here? And how can we ever understand them?

Through the shelves I watched people gather over an Isolette in the next pod. First the baby's own nurse, then another from the pod; next, when one of them went off to get her, a nurse who appeared to be in charge; finally, moments later, the young man in lab coat and Nikes who'd earlier been standing at the desk in front. Various alarms had begun sounding—buzzers, bells, blats—as the young man looked up at the monitors one last time, reached for a transparent green bag at bedside, and said loudly: ''Call it.'' Overhead, a page started: *Stat to neonatal intensive care, all attendings.* He put a part of the bag over the baby's face and began squeezing it rapidly.

Then I could see no more as workers surrounded the Isolette.

''Sir, I'm afraid I'll have to ask you to step out,'' Debbie said. She stood and placed Andrew back in his open crib. The child's eyes followed her as she walked away. He didn't cry.

I filed out alongside skittish new fathers, smiling grandparents, a couple of mothers still in hospital gowns and moving slowly, hands pressed flat against their stomachs. An X-ray machine bore down on us through the double doors and lumbered along the hallway, banging walls and scattering linen hampers, trashcans, supply carts. Where's this one? the tech asked. Pod 2, Mrs. Heslip told him.

Most of the others, abuzz with rumor, clustered just outside the doors. Some decided to call it a night and went on to the elevators across the hall, where I knew from experience they'd wait a while. I found stairs at the end of a seemingly deserted hall and went down them (they smelled of stale cigarettes and urine) into the kind of cool, gentle rain we rarely see back in New Orleans. There, when it comes, it comes hard and fast, making sidewalks steam, beating down banana trees and shucking leaves off magnolias, pouring over the edges of roofs and out of gutters that can't handle the sudden deluge.

I turned up the collar of my old tan sportcoat as I stepped out of the hospital doorway just in time to get splashed by a pickup that swerved toward the puddle when it saw me. I heard cackling laughter from inside.

Earlier I had noticed a small café on the corner a few blocks over. Nick's, Rick's, something like that, the whole front of it plate glass, with handwritten ads for specials taped to the glass and an old-style diner's counter. I decided to give it a try and headed that way. Moving through the streets of the rural South I'd fled a long time ago. Bessie Smith had died not too far from here, over around Clarksdale, when the white hospital wouldn't treat her following a car accident and she bled to death on the way to the colored one.

At age sixteen, I had fled. Fled my father's docility and sudden rages, fled old black men saying "mister" to ten-year-old white kids, fled the fields and the tire factory pouring thick black smoke out onto the whole town like a syrup, fled all those faces gouged out and baked hard and dry like the land itself. I had gone to the city, to New Orleans, and made a life of my own, not a life I was especially proud of, but mine nonetheless, and I'd always avoided going back. I'd avoided a lot of things. And now they were all waiting for me.

2

A FEW WEEKS BEFORE THAT, AT NINE IN THE MORNING, I'd just finished putting a friend's son on the bus to send him home. He'd kind of got himself lost in New Orleans, and I'd kind of found him, and I think finally we were all kind of glad, parent, child and myself, that I could still do the work. It was a beautiful morning, unseasonably cool, and I decided to walk home. So I left the Greyhound Terminal and started up Simon Bolivar, with downtown New Orleans (what they're now calling the CBD, for Central Business District) looming at my back like so many cliffs.

I never have figured out just how a street in this part of the city got named for a South American liberator, but that's New Orleans. Some of the streets down here actually have double signs, a regular-size one and a smaller one riding piggyback, with different names. Further up, where it becomes La Salle, Simon Bolivar has one of those.

I walked past the projects. Newer ones of slab and plastic looking like cheap college dorms from the fifties, older brick-and-cement ones like World War II institutional housing, most of them with sagging porches, window frames and entryways, air conditioners propped on long boards, spray-painted lovers' names or exhortations to *Try Jesus* on the walls. Then, crossing Martin Luther King, I passed the old Leidenheimer Bakery and a lengthy stretch of weathered Creole cottages and doubles, storefront churches, windowless corner foodstores. Every couple of blocks there were clusters of chairs and

crates beneath trees on the neutral ground where the
community's social life is carried on. Lots of boarded-
up buildings with signs on them. *Do Not Enter, No Ad-
mittance, Property Pelican Management.* There were
even signs on the Dumpsters outside the projects: *Prop.
of HANO.* Signs on everything. The ones we read, and
the ones we just know are there. We learn.

I went on up to Louisiana, turned left, looked in the
window at Brown Sugar Records and across at the Sand-
piper's sign over the door, a two-foot-high martini glass
complete with stirrer and olive and a rainbow arcing into
the glass. It's supposed to be lit up, of course, probably
all greens and blues, but the lights haven't worked in
twenty years at least. These great old signs still turn up
all over the city. Things are slow to change here, or
don't change at all.

I went on across St. Charles to Prytania, stopped at
the Bluebird for coffee, and stepped through my front
door just as the rain began. First a few scattered drops—
then a downpour so hard you could see and hear little
else.

Fifteen minutes later, the sun was struggling back out.

I poured an Abita into an oversized glass and settled
down by the window to look over notes on Camus and
Claude Simon. It was my semester to teach Modern
French Novel, something that rotated ''irregularly''
among our three full-time professors (who got benefits)
and four part-time instructors (no benefits: administra-
tion would be ecstatic if *everyone* were part-time), and
it had been a while. My last couple of books had done
well, and I hadn't been teaching much. But then I started
missing it. Also, I couldn't seem to get started on a new
book. I'd begun two or three, but they kept sounding
more like me—*my* ideas, the way *I* see things—than like
whatever character I supposedly was writing about.

Aujourd'hui, maman est morte.

That great opening line of the novel I probably admire
more than any other I've read. And I thought again how

much blunter, how much more matter-of-fact and drained of passion the phrase is in French than it ever could be in our own language. How well it introduces this voice without past or future, without history or anticipation, with only a kind of eternal, changeless present; how Meursault, and finally the novel itself, becomes a witness upon whom only detail (sunlight, sand, random clusters of events) registers. Telling in the calmest way possible this astonishing story of a man sentenced to death because he failed to cry at his mother's funeral.

I remembered, as I always did now, reading this, the telegrams Mother had sent, one before, one after, when my father was dying.

Afloat in reverie, I'd been distractedly watching a man make his way over the buckling sidewalk beneath an ancient oak tree opposite, and when now he turned to cross the street, I took notice.

Moments later, my doorbell chirred.

In the stories, Sherlock Holmes is forever watching people approach (and often hesitate) in the street below, and by the time they're at the door ringing for Mrs. Hudson he has already deduced from carriage, dress and general appearance just who they are and pretty much why they've come.

I, on the other hand, had absolutely no idea why this man was here.

"Mr. Griffin," he said when I opened the door. Still wearing, or wearing again, the suit he'd had on last week. It hadn't looked too good then. The tie was gone, though. "I hope I'm not interrupting anything, and I apologize for coming into your home like this. I'm—"

"I know who you are."

At his look of surprise, I said: "Hey. I'm a detective."

"Oh." As if that, indeed, explained it.

"And of course, as a writer, an inveterate snoop as well."

That was true enough. Sometimes sitting in restaurants or bars I'd become so engrossed in eavesdropping that I'd completely lose track of what my companion was saying. LaVerne had always just sat quietly, waiting for me to come back.

"Oh." A perfunctory smile.

"Actually, I saw you two out together a few times. The Camellia, Commander's, like that." Only a partial lie.

"Then you should've come over, said hello."

I shook my head.

"I know what she meant to you, Griffin. What you meant to one another."

He didn't. But he was a hell of a man for coming here to tell me that.

"You want a drink? Coffee or something?"

"Whatever you're having."

"Well, I tell you. What I've been having is this fine beer made out of hominy grits or somesuch right here in Governor Edwards's own state. But what I'd really like is a cup of *café au lait*. One so muddy and dark you think there've got to be catfish down in there somewhere. You in a hurry?"

"Not really."

"Then I'll make us a pot. What the hell."

He followed me out to the kitchen, staring with fascination at shelves of canned food and two-year-old coupons stuck under magnets on the refrigerator door, rifling the pages of surreptitious cookbooks, fingering the unholy contents of a spice rack.

"I don't know why I'm here," he told me when the coffee was ready and we were back by the window, he in a beat-up old wingback, me in my usual white wood rocker. "I mean, I *know;* but I don't know how to *tell* you."

He sipped coffee. From his expression it was, in miniature, everything he had hoped for from life.

"You and LaVerne, you were together a long time."

He looked at me. After a moment I nodded.

"We weren't." He looked down. I thought of a Sonny Boy Williamson song: *Been gone so long, the carpet's half faded on the floor*. Or possibly it was *carpets have faded*—hard to tell. Though mine were hardwood. "What I mean is," he said.

And we sat there.

"Yeah," I said finally. I got up and put on more milk to heat, poured us both refills when it was steaming, settled back. My rocker creaked on the floorboards.

"I don't know," he said. "We got together pretty far along in life. I sure didn't think there was anyone like LaVerne out there for me, not anymore. All that stuff about candlelight and the perfect mate and little bells going off, that's what you believe when you're nineteen or twenty maybe, some of us anyway. Then you get a few years on you and you realize that's not the way the world is at all, that's just not how it goes about its business. But still, one day there she was."

He looked up at me and his eyes were unguarded, open. "I hardly knew her, Lew. Less than a year. I loved her so much. Sure, I know an awful lot's gone under the bridge, for both of us, but I still think we'll have some time, you know? Then one day I look around and she just isn't there anymore. Like I'm halfway into this terribly important sentence I've waited a long time to say and I suddenly realize no one is listening. I don't know. Maybe I've been hoping somehow I'd be able to see LaVerne through your eyes, have more time with her, find out more about her, that way. Stupid, right?"

"No. Not stupid at all. That's what people are all about. That's something we can do for one another. We always get together to bury our dead. And then to bring them back, to remember what their lives were like, afterwards. Though Verne's life wasn't one either you or I can easily know or imagine."

He nodded.

"Good. You have to know that before you can know

anything else. But I just don't see what you want me to tell you. That she loved you? She must have, and you must know it. That it's terrible how she was taken from you? Hell, of course it is, man. Join the fucking club.''

"You think—'' he started, then took another draw of coffee. "I'm sorry. I haven't made myself at all clear. I didn't come here for assurances, however much I could use them just now. And yes, I know LaVerne loved me.'' He looked up from his cup. "Just as she did you, Lew.''

Something grabbed my throat and wouldn't let go. I swallowed coffee. It didn't help much.

"There have to be a lot of reasons why I came here. Maybe there'll be a time to sort them all out later. But primarily I came here to hire you.''

"Hire me?'' I said. It sounded more like *hrm*.

"I need a detective, Lew. A good one.''

"I don't do that anymore. Hell, I never did it very much. I sat in bars and drank, and eventually guys I was looking for would stumble by and trip over my feet. I'm a teacher now.''

"And a writer.''

"Yeah, well, that too. Once you've lost your pride, it gets easier, you know: you'll do almost any damned thing. You start off small, a piece for the local paper, or maybe this tiny little story about growing up, something like that. That's how they hook you. Then before you know it, you're writing a series for them.''

"Yeah. Yeah, LaVerne told me a thing or two about your pride.''

"Which in my particular case went *after* a fall.''

"And I read your books, Lew. All of them.''

"Then you must be one hell of a man for sure. Don't know if *I* could do it.''

"Yeah,'' he said, placing cup and saucer on the floor beside him and waving off my tacit offer of more. Some people still know how to let a good thing be. "You wanta stop pushing me away here, Lew? 'S'not much about this whole thing that's funny. You know?''

I shook my head. Not disputing him: agreeing. The invisible something eased off on my throat and went back to its dark corner.

"I'm listening," I said.

"Good." He took a cream-colored envelope out of his inside breast pocket and held it, edge-down like a blade, against one thigh. "You know anything about LaVerne having a kid?''

"She never had any. Always told me she couldn't.''

"Not only could, it seems, but also did. Back when she was married to Horace Guidry—''

"Her doctor.''

He nodded. "Went on fertility drugs or something, I guess, when he kept insisting. Then when they split, I guess he got full custody, no visitation. Even a restraining order.''

"In consideration of the respondent's unwholesome past, no doubt.''

"And of the petitioner's large sums of money and standing in the community, right. You got it.''

"Why would she never have said anything?''

"I asked her that once, when she first told me. She couldn't say. But I think maybe it was kind of like she shut that door completely—like she had to, just to keep on getting by. Know what I mean?''

I did. I also knew that winds have a way of coming out of nowhere and blowing those doors open again.

We sat there silently a moment and he said, "Yeah, I guess we don't ever know anybody as well as we think we do, huh?''

"I'm beginning to think we don't ever know anyone at all.''

"Yeah. Well anyway, we're sitting in Burger King one night, we'd been together seven or eight months by then, and LaVerne looks across at me between bites and she says: I've got a kid, you know. Talk about getting hit by a semi. And she proceeds to tell me all about it, right there and then, with these teenage kids blowing wrappers off straws at each other in the next booth. So what you think I should do about it? she asks me afterward. What you wanta do? I say. And she goes: I think maybe I have to try and talk to her, Chip. I think I want my daughter to know who her mother was. Cause of course she'd be like eighteen now, able to make her own decisions about things like this. And the stuff LaVerne saw every day at that shelter she was working at, it had to make her think about all that. Parents and children, husbands and wives, all the things they can do to one another. About being all alone, too.''

"You find her?"

"We started looking. Retained a lawyer to contact the father—"

"Anything there?"

"Damn little. Lots of fast footwork from *his* lawyers. Including, as I understand it, a brief admonitory call from a judge.''

"I take it, then, that the girl—what's her name?"

"Alouette. We're not sure what last name she's using.''

"I take it she's not with the father. With Guidry.''

"Apparently not for some time. And short of a court order, which wasn't about to happen, that's pretty much all we could get out of the good doctor's lawyers. Then finally our own lawyer suggested we might want to get in touch with a PI out in Metairie, a guy who specializes in finding people—"

"Who was that?"

"A. C. Boudleaux.''

"Achille. I know him. He come up with anything? If he didn't, you might as well hang it on the line, 'cause nobody else will either. He's good.''

"Here's his report.'' He handed over the envelope. "It's not much, but he was only on it for a couple weeks. Then LaVerne . . . Well, you know what happened. And that kind of ate up most of the money I had left. Don't ever let anybody tell you medical insurance is good for shit, cause it ain't, not when the time comes you need it. Besides, nothing else much seemed to matter then but her. Not that I could really do anything for her.''

"So now you're trying to do exactly that.''

"Do something for her, you mean. Yeah. I guess. What the hell else is there? If it's money you're thinking about, how I'm gonna pay you, don't worry. I'll get it. I always manage.''

I'd been looking through the contents of the envelope as he spoke. There wasn't much, but it proved enough to wash this reluctant Sinbad up, days later, on the foreign shores of the Mississippi. Nigger Lew looking around, and no raft or Huck anywhere in sight.

"I don't want your money,'' I told him.

"What, then?''

"How about a sandwich and a beer or two, for a start. On me.''

"You drive a hard bargain, Griffin.''

"Okay, I'm flexible. *You* buy.''

THE NOVEL'S TRUE PROTAGONIST, I TELL MY STUDENTS, is always time. With the years, it's gotten somewhat easier to say things like that without immediately looking over my shoulder or down at the floor. And *then*, of course, you go on and talk about the flow of time in Proust, about Faulkner's sequestrations of history, about the abrogation of time *and* history in Beckett.

So by commodious vicus (you all know the tune: feel free to sing along) we arrive now at a point one week before Chip Landrieu showed up like an orphan at my doorstep, this being *three* weeks before I stood watching someone repast on chips and cola from a trashcan in Mississippi.

Everybody with me so far?

Nine in the morning, then. I was sitting in that same white rocker with a bottle of Courvoisier on the floor alongside and an espresso cup in hand. I'd gone from beer to scotch to the strongest thing I had. I hadn't been able to find anything like a proper glass but figured the cup would do.

Some people have aquariums, into which they stare for hours. Here in New Orleans, we have patios. And in those patios, likely as not, we have banana trees. Lots of banana trees if we're not careful, because they grow almost while you watch. The parts you see are shoots off the real tree underground, and there's not much to them: just an awful lot of water bound in honeycombs of thin tissue, topped by enormous leaves the wind shreds to green fringe. They'll go down with a single hard swipe from a machete (looking in cross section much like celery stalks), but a week later there'll be two more already shooting up, two or three feet high.

Squirrels here seem virtually to live off these trees. They hang upside down like bats (or, for that matter, like the fruit itself) and dine from bunches of ripe bananas; then when those are gone, smaller, green ones; and finally the bright red blooms. Littering the patio floor with a continuous fall of shredded banana, peel, leaf, bloom. The squirrels are scrawny gray ones with tattered, sketchy tails, not at all like the plume-tailed red squirrels of my Arkansas childhood.

Life's not anything here if it's not adaptable. And relentless. A year or so after I first came to New Orleans, I took a snapshot of the old camelback shotgun on Dryades where I was living with four or five other guys and a couple of families, and was surprised to see how green everything was. Not just trees and grass, but wooden stairs, the edges of beveled glass in doors and windows, cracks in painted walls, balcony railings, sidewalks where air conditioners dripped—as though a fine film of green had settled over the entire world. And I had gotten so used to it that I didn't see it anymore, until that snapshot saw it again for me.

I was still sitting there sipping Courvoisier, thinking about life's adaptability and musing further upon the fact that "seeing again" is finally what art's all about, when my doorbell chirred. Almost before it stopped, there was a pounding at the door. And then before I could get to it, the door opened.

"Lock your fucking door, Lew," Walsh said, closing it behind him. "Where the hell you think you live?"

I sat back down. "Don't you have criminals you ought to be out there catching or something?"

"They'll still be there. Always have been. So's the goddamn paperwork. You got any coffee?"

"I can make you some."

"Don't bother. Probably had too much already."

He went out to the kitchen for a Diet Coke, came back and sank into the wingback's tired embrace, looking for a hard moment at the bottle on the floor, the cup in my hand.

"Goddamn it, Lew, what the fuck are you doing here, anyway? You oughta be at the church already. You got people up there waiting for you. You just sitting here getting drunk, that it? Business as usual?"

"Nope. He's definitely not getting drunk, Don old friend. Not that he hasn't tried. Valiantly."

"So, what then? You're just gonna pretend it didn't happen? You gonna just blow off the whole thing, after all she meant to you? And after all the crap she put up with from you for all those years? Cause you didn't give her shit when she was alive, man, you know? You know that, I know you do. And it's damn little enough you can do now."

He leaned back, breathed deeply. Held up his empty can in a mock *salut*. "I'm sorry. I coulda said that better, I guess. Most things I could, these days."

"You scored the point, Don. It's okay."

He shook his head, looked out to the patio. "I don't know, Lew. Ever since Josie and the girls left, everything looks different. I don't know; I'm one hell of a guy to be giving advice. But sometimes it seems to me like you spend half your life doing everything you can to avoid things and the rest trying to make up for it. I have trouble understanding that. Always have."

"So you got another point to make?"

"Well, I got this point that you better get up off your butt and haul that same sorry thing on over to Verne's goddamn funeral. That's the only other point I got. For now, anyway."

"I'm not going, Don. I can't."

"Lew." He sat back again, exhaled deeply. "Listen to me. I swear it, Lew: you're going. If I have to get a squad down here and have 'em help me drag you into that church, you're going. You hear what I'm telling you?"

"Such devotion and friendship's a rare thing."

"Yeah, Lew, it is. It sure as hell is. But what the fuck would you know about that?"

I looked at him then and felt tears force their way out onto my face.

Stones in my passway, as Robert Johnson said. And my road seem dark as night.

Surely the funeral could not have been conducted in silence—surely (to whatever recondite end) I've invented this—but in memory that is how I always see it: several dozen people sitting straight as fences on the hardwood pews, not a sound anywhere, even traffic sounds from outside curiously hushed and transformed as though broadcast from somewhere else, from another world or time, and people moving, when at last they began to do so, as though that silence were substantial, something that resisted, something they had to push through, slowing and drawing out their movements. As though we all had slipped unaware into some timeless deep.

I remembered James Baldwin's funeral a few years back. The solemn slow progress of cross and chasuble, and then, breaking over it, tearing that long European sentence apart, the sudden leap and skitter of African drums.

And that was just how the world came back, sudden, staccato, as Don and I stood on the steps outside the church.

"Where can I drop you, Lew?"

"I think I'll walk back. Maybe swing by the school."

"C'mon. It's five, six miles at least."

"I'll be fine, Don."

"No you won't. You haven't been fine more than ten minutes in all the years I've known you. But if you're saying you'll get through this, yeah, I guess you will.

You always do. Take care, friend. Buy you dinner some night?"

"Sounds good. I'll call you."

"No you won't, Lew. You'll mean to, but you won't do it. And then eventually I'll just come on over there and pry you out of the house and haul you off somewhere. Just like always."

He started away, shaking his head.

"Don . . ."

"Yeah?" Turning back. I had never noticed before this just how deeply the web of fine lines had sunk everywhere into his face, or that flesh now hung slack beneath chin and cheekbones. Even his eyes had a grayish cast to them.

"Thanks."

"Hey, don't embarrass me in front of Verne's friends. I hate it when you get all teary-eyed, I ever tell you that?"

"I mean it."

"Yeah. I know you do. I know that."

"You hear much from Josie?"

"Not so long as the checks keep coming. Shit, I don't mean that. She sends me pictures of the kids every few months. She's real good about doing that."

"She still loves you, Don."

"Yeah. Well. Guess I better go shut down a few crack houses, huh? Got a few hours left in the day. You sure you don't want a ride?"

"I'm sure."

He climbed into the Regal, his own, that he'd been driving at least ten years, waved to me in the rearview and hauled it into a lumbering U back toward downtown. The department kept offering him new official cars and he kept telling them his was fine, he was used to it.

I walked down State to Freret and turned right. Kids on bicycles heading to and from classes at Tulane or Loyola shot past me. I hadn't had a car since Vicky left.

At first I'd planned to buy one, but I kept putting it off for one reason or another, and after a while it just stopped being important. I'd got used to walking and liked it, and if I had to get somewhere I couldn't walk, well, cabs in New Orleans are plentiful as roaches.

I crossed Napoleon and, one street over, turned onto General Pershing. Blackjack Pershing, they called him. Most of his mounted troops were "buffalo soldiers." Black men. They performed so well that Pershing suggested only blacks should be taken into the armed services. Except for officers, of course.

Squirrels ran along power lines with blue jays screaming and swooping about them. It was garbage pickup day for this part of town; emptied plastic bins sat inverted or on their sides before most houses. This stretch was pure New Orleans, a jumble of wrought iron, balconies, leaded glass, gingerbread, Corinthian columns. Grand old homes well preserved, decaying ones once every bit as grand and now carved into multiple dwellings, simple raised cottages and bungalows.

I walked along thinking hard about Verne, and about something I'd read in an art journal, unable to sleep, at two or three that morning. The lives we lead, it said, the art or artifacts we produce, all these are but scrims, one layer over countless other layers, some that reveal, some that conceal.

Twenty-six years ago I killed a man. I was playing detective in those days, and I was pretty crazy back then too, so I guess I must have been trying on some half-imagined role as avenging angel. Like other roles I've tried, before and since, it didn't fit.

The thing is, I rarely think about it. Though from time to time, walking these shabby streets (especially at night, it seems), I'll glance into a stranger's face and something there, in his eye, takes me back. Dostoevski said that we're all guilty of everything. And while I never could bring myself to accept Christian notions of sin and atonement, there's definitely something to karma. The things we do pile up on us, weigh us down. Or hold us in place, at very least.

4

I TRIED TO CALL BOUDLEAUX AFTER READING THROUGH
the report, but his machine told me he was in Lafayette
on business and would be away "indeterminately." I
could have tried motels up there, but he was almost certainly staying with family. And that spread it pretty thin,
since one way or another he seemed to be related to just
about everyone in Lafayette *and* Evangeline parishes.

Six months old now, the report was, like all his reports, thorough, concise and poorly spelled, typed on a
Royal portable he'd had since college and to every appearance never once cleaned in all that time, *e*'s and *o*'s
indistinguishable, *a*'s little blobs of ink atop frail curved
spines. And valuable, like most documents, as much for
what it did not say as for what it did.

The map is not the territory. The limits of your language are the limits of your world. Catchphrases from
the fifties and from circa 1921.

Apparently Alouette, as Boudleaux discovered (hard
upon stone-walling from Guidry and a pride of lawyers,
and a call from that same judge, who casually inquired
concerning the status of his PI license), had not been in
her father's home for some time.

Early spring of last year, one of her teachers, Mr.
Sacher, homeroom and American history, began report-
ing her as nonattendant. Per procedure, he notified his
supervisor and principal and attempted, on his own, to
reach Alouette or her parents at the phone number listed
in school files. Repeatedly, there was no answer at this
number. Nor does any record of administrative response

exist, though the principal is certain that he and Mr. Sacher "discussed the matter."

Parents were listed in Alouette's file as Horace and L. Guidry, and above *Occupation* (the forms were filled out by the students themselves) was entered *Fuzzician*. Sacher checked the phone book and found no home number (assuming it was unlisted) but in the yellow pages a *Horace Guidry, Internist,* with offices in the Touro area. When he called and finally talked his way past the receptionist and a nurse, Dr. Guidry listened a moment and told him he would have to get back to him. And when, later that afternoon, he did, it was by way of a conference call, their two phones looped into an intercom phone at the downtown offices of Bordelon, Bordelon and Schmidt.

Stating his concern, Sacher was informed by one of the lawyers that Alouette had upon her own volition and without notice, some weeks previously, departed her father's board and care. Her present whereabouts were unknown, though efforts were still under way to locate her.

Had there been family difficulties? Sacher asked. Was Alouette under any unusual pressures?

You are her teacher, am I correct? a third voice inquired. And upon Sacher's assent, went on: Then I'm afraid I see no compelling or appropriate reason for us to answer such inquiry.

Boudleaux had found his way to Mr. Sacher within three hours of being engaged by Chip Landrieu. As it happened, he had a couple of cousins who worked in the mailroom at Bordelon, Bordelon and Schmidt. And so, not long after closing that same day, a Friday, Boudleaux knew what there was in B, B&S's file concerning Alouette. Which wasn't much.

Following a couple of practice runs, absences of two or three days the first time, then several weeks, from both of which she returned properly sorrowful and acquiescent, one Tuesday morning she headed off to school and to all appearances fell through a rabbit hole. Police were properly notified. Friends interviewed. Malls, clubs and other teenage water holes scouted. All to no avail.

The Guidrys had themselves engaged a local agency, South-East Investigations, to conduct a search for the girl. Clyde South and Michelle East were married, and Boudleaux knew them both. They were running into stone walls too.

To his report Boudleaux had appended a list of others he'd interviewed and (before being taken off the case) planned to.

On second or third reading, one of the attributions caught my eye. *Counselor,* it gave as occupation, then: *Foucher Women's Shelter.* Where Verne had been working the last few years. The name above was *Juan Garces.*

I called to be sure he was in, then walked over to Tchoupitoulas and grabbed a White Fleet cab. An elderly woman behind a minuscule desk in the lobby (it had once been the foyer where residents had mailboxes, and I hope there weren't too many of them) directed me upstairs.

He was sitting before a computer monitor and swiveled partway around, hands staying on the keys, when, in the absence of a door, I knocked at the frame. He swung back to the keyboard, hit Save and Exit, came all the way back and got up. We shook hands.

"Sorry," he said. "But you have to do what they want you to. You must be Mr. Griffin." He waved me into a chair.

Uneven stacks of folders and stapled papers all but covered the table space around keyboard and computer. To the right at shoulder level, beside a narrow window, a plastic board was lined with yellow Post-It notes in a tiny blue script. Garces reached over and peeled off the top one, dropped it into the trashcan under the desk. The other wall was taken over, above, by a reproduction of

Matisse's *Blue Frog/Yellow Nude* (or is it the other way around? I can never remember) and, below, by a shelf of books running to Robert Pirsig, Genet, Laing and Szasz. I took note of Delany's *Dhalgren* and *The Motion of Light in Water.*

Garces was fair-skinned with light blue eyes, and somehow gave the impression of being short and gangly at the same time. His dark hair was close-cropped. He wore a black T-shirt, pressed slacks, a linen sportcoat with the sleeves turned up a couple of times, cordovan loafers without socks. Fortyish.

"So what is it that I can help you with, Mr. Griffin? Something to do with a friend, you said on the phone."

"LaVerne Landrieu."

"Of course," he said after a moment. "You're Lewis: *that* Griffin. I didn't connect, when you gave me your name earlier. I'm sorry, Mr. Griffin—"

"Lew."

"Lew. It's a loss to us all, you know. She made a difference in a lot of lives around here. But you must know that."

"No. I don't."

"Oh. But whenever she spoke of you . . . You two haven't been in touch, then?"

I shook my head.

"I'm sorry. I didn't know. Do you mind my asking if there was any particular reason for that?"

"What I keep telling myself is that I didn't think her marriage needed ghosts like me showing up on the stairs."

"Did you meet Chip Landrieu?"

"Afterwards, yes."

He nodded. "Things so often happen in the wrong order in our lives."

"How well did you know Verne, Mr. Garces?"

"Richard."

I pointed inquiringly back toward the doorframe, the name plaque beside it.

"No one outside my family ever calls me Juan. And no one, period, calls me Mr. Garces. But I'm afraid I don't understand."

"I mean, did the two of you ever talk? About personal things."

He shook his head. "I'm sorry. Once I found out who you were, I naturally assumed . . . We really should start this whole encounter again from scratch, I think. I assumed you knew LaVerne and I were close. That this was why you came here."

The phone buzzed. He excused himself, picked it up, listened for a moment, then responded in Spanish that was far too rapid for me to follow. He hung up and penned a note that he added to the board.

"Over the years LaVerne and I became good friends, yes. It happened slowly, very slowly, and without either of us planning or even expecting it. People have always come to me to talk, that's kind of how I got into all this. But that's as far as it ever goes. And LaVerne was one to keep her distance; you knew that when you first talked to her. We were both private people. Never mixed much socially with those we work with. Try to keep it professional."

"But you and Verne. . . . "

"Yeah, and it was funny. *I*'d always been the one to listen. But after a while—we'd go out for coffee after work, or sometimes later on we'd meet for breakfast in the morning—I found myself babbling on and on about *my* problems, *my* previous or current live-in. Or my relationship with my parents, for God's sake. That had never happened before, and I've been doing this work for a long time. Then one morning when the plates have been cleared and we're sitting there over a final cup of coffee she says to me: I want to tell you about my life, I want someone to know all this."

"People here didn't know?"

"What they knew was that this woman had paid her dues at one of the country's toughest rape centers, and

then on her own she had gone back to school and got a
degree in psychology and now here she was, twelve or
fourteen hours a day sometimes. That's all they had to
know.''

He looked briefly out the window. A jay screamed as
it swept across the pane and out of sight.

''I listen, sometimes all day and part of the night, to
people's problems. I know what it's like out there, and
how little I can do. One of my clients, last month her
boyfriend fucked their year-old daughter and then
slammed her headfirst against the wall 'so she wouldn't
tell.' I've got pregnant mothers trying to live out of
Dumpsters and a shopping cart. And husbands or parents
swooping in all the time with their lawyers and threats
trying to take my clients' kids away, always with this
same attitude, like if I just'll listen to them, I'll know
what's right. I don't know what's right, Lew.''

He looked back at me. ''I'm sorry. A little off track
there. But there are days, and this is one of them, when
I have to wonder what my place really is in all this.''

''I understand.''

''Yeah. You pretty much lived it, LaVerne said.''

''Not anymore.''

''Well. Maybe not. Not on the surface, anyway.''

I thought of a review of my third novel, published in
a small magazine specializing in mysteries. I've had doz-
ens of bad reviews, most of them justified, I'm sure, but
that was the only one I ever felt unfair. Cadging personal
details from my publisher and a common acquaintance,
the reviewer proceeded to ignore my novel and instead
to review me, claiming that *Black Hornet* was nothing
more than a record, a document, of my personal failures.

Maybe that reviewer was right. And maybe Richard
Garces was right, too. Who knows what evil . . . ? Well,
the Shadow do. Or he be sposed to, at any rate.

''Over the next months,'' Garces went on, ''LaVerne
told me what I guess must be her whole life story. Even
for me, I have to say, it was something of a revelation.

And then, to think that she could come through all that and arrive where she did.''

"She was rather an amazing woman."

"I don't think any of us ever quite realized *how* amazing."

"We don't, usually. Not till afterwards. Things happening in the wrong order, like you say."

"Yeah." We were both quiet a moment. "She told me one night how she waited for you for over two hours outside, what was it, a bus station? Your friend from Paris—"

"Vicky."

"—had just gotten on the plane to go back, and I guess this was a little after LaVerne and Guidry split up, when she'd already been working rape-crisis for a while. You hadn't seen each other, I guess, for a long time by then, and she went down there without any idea what to expect, how you'd react. Or even how she felt about it all herself."

" 'Whatever works. You wait and see.' "

"Right. And she told me that that was maybe the hardest thing she'd ever done in her life. That she'd never been more afraid than she was that night, and the next few days. I don't know. But that story has really stayed with me. Whenever I think about making decisions, really hard ones, I still think about that."

"She ever talk much about when she and Guidry were together?"

He shook his head. "That whole period was kind of walled off. She did once tell me that the whole time she was married to Dr. Guidry she felt she was masked, as for Mardi Gras, and that no one would ever be able to see who she really was, however closely they looked. I remember thinking it was something like the way people remember war experiences: these brief, incredibly concentrated periods of time that become central to their lives and all-consuming, but then that time's gone and the experiences are essentially meaningless in the everyday practical world around them, and they let them go. Except in a way I guess LaVerne was talking about a period of peace, surrounded by war.''

''You sure of that?''

''Which part?''

''The peace part.''

''You mean, was the period as tranquil as it appeared?''

''Right.''

''Few periods are, really—even after our memory's got to work on them. But I more or less felt she wanted somehow to preserve that time, keep it apart. Pure, in a manner of speaking.''

''Maybe so. But she and Guidry split, not at all too peacefully from what little I know. So what happened? Did they get along? Were there problems between them, even early on?''

Garces shrugged. ''The book's closed.''

''So maybe we'll have to go see the movie.''

I stood and thanked him for his time and help. Then in a time-honored tradition stretching back from Columbo at least to Porfiry Petrovich, I thought of one more thing. ''So why do you think LaVerne wouldn't talk about that period with you, when she talked about everything else?''

''I really don't know any more than I've told you.''

''Was there something different about it? Not just that she was chasing the American Dream and it almost caught her. But something—I don't know—traumatic, maybe?''

He hesitated, but when he glanced at me then, we both knew.

''You mean her daughter.''

I nodded. He exhaled.

''I'm sorry, I wasn't trying to mislead you. Hell, of course I was; nothing else I can call it. But LaVerne had told me you didn't know about Alouette. She didn't talk

about her very much herself. I guess things hadn't gone
well for a long time."

"And then they didn't go at all."

"Yeah, that's pretty much it."

"Did you know LaVerne had tried to get in touch
with her daughter? To see her?"

"No, she never told me that. I know there were court
orders involved, at one time. Those would no longer
apply, of course. But LaVerne always said she wouldn't
contact her daughter, that it would be easier on Alouette
that way."

"She changed her mind. You know anything about
what the problems might have been between Verne and
the good doctor?"

"No, I'm sorry. Though I'm not certain I'd tell you
even if I did. If I thought I did, that is. There's a kind
of professional reflex at work here."

I thanked him again. I'd got almost out the door when
he said behind me: "You're trying to find Alouette, is
that it?"

I turned back. "Chip Landrieu asked me to. I figure
it's little enough."

"Yeah. Well, I could probably help you with that."

5

ONE OF THE FIRST THINGS I FELL IN LOVE WITH IN
New Orleans was its cemeteries. The house I lived in
on Dryades when I first came here had one nearby, a
block of gravesites smack in the middle of street after
street of houses and apartments, with a low brick wall
and, just beyond, a border of the tiers of vaults here
called ovens—all of it white and dazzling in the sunlight. There was at the same time such gravity and
such lightness to it; and ever since, when things
crowd too closely in upon me, I tend to head to the
cemeteries for a strange solace I find nowhere else.

The largest (though really it's a blur of many
smaller, distinct ones) is at Canal and City Park, a
wilderness of tombs stretching far into the distance, a
sprawling city of the dead. Many older crypts have
sunk almost completely into the ground. And above
them, as though reaching for sky, loom thickets of
crosses, angels, statues large and small, figures of
women shrouded in grief.

The oldest is on Basin Street, St. Louis Cemetery
No. 1, at what was long ago the edge of town and
later the edge of Storyville. Marie Laveau, Paul Mor-
phy and the city's first mayor dwell there now. Occu-
pying but a single square block, it's pure chaos: a
riot of twisted pathways that end as often as not in
cul-de-sacs. Tombs sit askew, at every conceivable
angle and tilt, the lower corners of many of them
wrenched free of the ground.

My personal favorite is on Washington. It fills two or three blocks in a well-decayed part of town, chockful of gravesites in a bewildering jumble of styles, size and age, cut through by narrow, corridor-like paths, yet in its own way rigidly symmetrical: disorder's cur brought to heel. Whenever I'm down that way, I make a point of going by.

Which I did that afternoon on the way home, wandering its pathways for half an hour or more, reading off names at random. Intimate stories began unfurling. Then I moved on to the next, or the one after.

Finally I left and ambled along Washington. Stopped off at a corner grocery for a quick po-boy and beer. Took the beer with me to finish as I walked up La Salle, jagging from sidewalk (where there was one) to street (where there wasn't, or where, from blockage or a quakelike upheaval of tree roots, it proved impassable).

A couple of blocks up, I turned into an alley between shoulder-to-shoulder doubles to trash the Dixie bottle. Most of the places along here seemed to be occupied—presumptive Christmas decorations hung on some abbreviated porches, leftover Halloween skeletons on one—but the houses either side of this particular alley, for whatever reasons, had been scuttled. One, to the left, once lime-green, had all windows and doors boarded over; its yellowish neighbor lacked windows and doors entirely and was heaped with refuse ranging from rotting lumber and linoleum to remains of impromptu parties (fast-food bags, bottles, candles) and grocery sacks of garbage, perhaps from adjoining quarters.

I lifted the lid of one of the bins, *La Salle* painted on in red, and saw just beyond, at the back of the alley against the latticework wall, a body. A woman's, I confirmed, stepping closer. She lay face-down, skirt thrown up over back and head. Pale, bloody rump in open air.

Twentyish, I decided, after turning her over. And

dead. Possibly from a blow to the head: temples were
spongy, eyes pushed forward and swollen. Possibly
from a knife held against the neck as they butt-raped
her, nicking a carotid.

Not that it mattered.

I knocked on the nearest occupied door, pushed my
way in before the woman who answered could protest
or ask questions, and dialed 911.

"Walsh," I told them.

"We'll have to get your name, number and loca-
tion," the guy said.

"Walsh—or I hang up. There's a body. *You* decide."

Two minutes later, Don was on the line.

I spent an hour or so answering the usual array of
police-type questions to at least three different groups
of people, then went home. Later that night I sat with
a glass of gin, neat, one of my own books face-down,
unheeded, against my thigh, open to a particularly violent scene. I didn't need to read it, I knew it—by
heart, as they used to say.

For years now, sequestered in this house, the one
Vicky and I lived in together, the one Verne often
visited, I had written book after book about street
life, crime, about violence both random and purposeful, about frustration and despair and, occasionally,
vengeance. But what I wrote, all those supposed "realistic" scenes, were only a kind of nostalgia, a ro-
mancification, sheerest dissembling; I could never
portray what it was really like out there.

It wasn't that, in the years of my retreat, violence
and pain had grown; but that I myself, believing I
understood, believing I was saying important things,
huddled down there, had steadily grown smaller.

I did not and do not understand. I will never understand.

THEY NEVER REALLY KNEW WHAT HAPPENED TO CLARE Fellman.

One morning in late October she'd been conjugating the verb *parler* for her first-period students and suddenly, between first- and second-person *présent du subjonctif*, she was on the floor, unconscious, all sensation and control (as she would discover, three days later, upon waking) gone from her body's right side. Because they didn't know what else to call it, after sending her off on numerous day trips through CAT scanners and MRI's and the like, the doctors at Oschner called it a CVA.

She was twenty-two at the time. Now she was thirty-six.

Nothing much ever came back to that right side. Over the next year, first at Oschner, then at a rehab hospital near Covington, she had painstakingly learned again to reach and pick up things and hold on to them, to guide a spoon from lift-off to touchdown through the uncertain space between planets of bowl and mouth, to negotiate the fall between chair and bed and wheelchair and toilet, and finally to walk. Life had become all new conjunctions for her, she told me: impossible joinings and connections others took for granted. She still wears braces at knee and ankle, canvas with Velcro these days, and a slight drag in her gait shows the extra focus required whenever that side is called on. It reminds me, oddly enough, of the way a jazz player, confronted with straight eighth notes, instinctively drags them out into dotted eighths and sixteenths.

Her speech, too, bears the mark of having been re-learned. She speaks slowly, carefully, as though each word carries in its wake its own small period, filling the spaces with quick smiles and, often, with laughter that seems as much at her own halting progress as at any-thing else.

We'd met a year or so back at an Alliance Française event, a special showing of a film version of *L'Étranger* and buffet dinner after, to which I'd gone with Tony (Antoine, but don't dare use it) Roppolo, one of our English Department adjuncts. Absolutely guarantee you the stinkiest cheeses imaginable, Tony told me. And how could a guy pass up a thing like that?

Moments before the film began, Clare sank into the aisle seat beside me; Tony leaned forward for a quick hello and brief introduction. She held out her left hand and I took it, somewhat awkwardly, with my right. Afterwards we all sat at one of the long folding tables shuffling morsels of Cheshire, Brie and Camembert in among careful mouthsful of wine. By the time we'd switched from nouveau Beaujolais to a dark, ripe cab-ernet (Kool-Aid! she had exclaimed with her first sip of the Beaujolais) and Tony had washed out to sea (where periodically we caught sight of him bobbing here and there among bodies) Clare and I were well on our way to becoming (as she put it) new best friends.

For a time then, things moved pretty quickly, certainly far more quickly than made any kind of decent good sense. We were both old enough and, I'm sure, in our own ways damaged enough to know better. Nor did either of us, I think, really anticipate or intend what hap-pened.

Then over the last couple of months, breathless and blinking, and with no clearer resolve or culpability than that with which we began, we'd found ourselves pulling back from one another. Too many unasked questions between us, maybe; too many wartime raids and too little faith in the cease-fire. Sometimes sitting beside Clare I felt as though unsaid things were growing like vines all around us, filling the room.

Of course, I felt that way with most of the people close to me.

And I was surprised, returning home from the Foucher shelter and my cemetery stroll, to find a message from her on my machine.

It's Clare, Lew. The spaces between her words were chinked with the tape's quiet hissing, anonymous background sounds. *Yeah, me. I'm sorry to bother you. I know about LaVerne, and I'm so sorry. If there's anything I can do, just let me know. But I have a friend who's got a problem, and I thought you might be able to help.* A pause. *Could you call me when you get a chance? Please?*

She answered, breathing hard, after six or seven rings.

"Lew. Thanks for calling back. Give me a minute, okay? I was doing my rehab stuff."

Threaded on the phone's fine silver nerve, we hung there. I listened as her breathing slowed.

"Okay, thanks. I know this is a bad time."

"Something about a friend, you said."

"Sheryl Silva. She works in dietary at the school and usually takes her break when I do, right before lunchtime. For her it's a little island of peace between preparation and storm. And after three straight periods, the last one my honors group, I'm pretty desperate. I try to stay away from the teachers' lounge, which is mostly bitching and conversations about children or new refrigerators, neither of which I have or expect to. So there'd just be the two of us there in the lunchroom, and after a while we fell into the habit of sitting together. Though a lot of the time we wouldn't say much of anything. Just sit there sipping iced tea, smiling vaguely at one another and looking out a window. Then last week she asks me if I'm 'married or anything.' I mean, we know abso-

lutely nothing about one another. And when I tell her
no, she asks me if I ever had a man beat me, or try to
hurt me. Says she has, when I tell her no, but she thought
that was all over.''

''And it isn't.''

''I think it's just threats, so far, from what she tells
me.''

''Husband?''

''I don't know. She wasn't too clear about that. They
lived together, at any rate.''

''Lived. You sure we're talking past tense here? *Le
passé simple?*''

For a moment I was flooded with a sense of unreality,
as though lights had dimmed and now I could see the
stage set around me for the insubstantial, trumped-up
thing it was, and knew the actors very soon must exit to
stage-left lives of lunch meat, arrogant children, cars
needing tires and new batteries. A cue card flipped up
in the back of my mind; or a prompter whispered beyond
the footlights. *This is none of your business, Griffin,
none of your business at all.* But I had a longtime habit
of ignoring scripted lines and improvising.

''Not for a while. I asked her what he'd done and she
just looked at me. And then, after a minute, she said:
Well, he put these dead chickens in my mailbox. And
on the back porch. Just kind of hung them out there, like
a string of peppers or garlic.''

''She black or white?''

''Latin.''

''Too bad. She be black, she know zackly what to do:
fry them suckers.''

''Very funny, Lew. Maybe I should hang up and call
Dr. Ruth instead. She probably knows a few tricks you
can do with chickens.''

''Might read you her favorite salivious, I mean las-
civious, passages from Frank Harris. Salacious? Man
had a way with geese, as I recall.''

''Look, this is the thing: You can talk to him, make

him see he's heading for real trouble if this goes on.''

"Man to man, hm?"

"Yeah, kind of."

"Well, Clare, I tell you. While it's true I used to do that sort of thing once in a while, it's also true that at the time I was twenty years younger and hadn't been riding my buns and a desk for six years straight. Be like all those almost hairless guys from the sixties trying to make their comeback as rock and rollers. I.e., ludicrous. Besides, all my tie-dye's at the cleaners.''

"Please, Lew. As a favor to me? How can you turn down a poor little crippled girl?''

"Oh. Well, since you put it like that."

"Then you'll do it?"

"I'll talk to the guy, Clare. Politely. And that's all. He says boo, I'm a ghost.''

"You're a jewel."

But when I looked in the mirror afterwards it wasn't sparkle I saw, more like a dullness that drew everything else to it. I remembered how old and used-up Walsh had looked to me the day of Verne's funeral. I couldn't be looking much better, and probably looked a hell of a lot worse. But enough of such reverie, I thought: there were things in the world that needed doing. Missions to be undertaken, wrongs to right, rights to champion.

Lew the Giant Killer.

SO AT MIDNIGHT OR THEREABOUTS, HERE I AM, WITH A list of this guy's habitats and less sense than your average lemming, prowling bars along Louisiana and Dryades looking for the chicken man.

Just like the good old days. Shut away from the world, the heady smell of piss and beer and barely contained fury all around me. And threading through it all, like a Wagnerian leitmotif, the quiet refrain: This is none of your business, Griffin, none at all.

I remembered a history professor back at LSUNO talking about the Russians' propensity for throwing themselves beneath tanks just to slow things down; saying that such irrational ferocities made them fearsome fighters.

But I was just going to talk to this guy, of course.

The Ave. Social & Pleasure Club was my tenth or twelfth try. I'd started at Henry's Soul Food and Pie Shop over on Claiborne and worked my way here.

It was a cinderblock affair, the butt half of a grocery whose painted-over windows advertised *Big Bo' Po-Boys* and *Fresh Seafood,* with an unbelievably crude painting of a crab holding a po-boy in its claws and (who would have thought it possible?) leering. The club, alas, didn't get such star treatment: only its name and a long arrow pointing to the single door.

Several underfed light bulbs hung here and there from the ceiling as though waiting for their mothers to come take them home. Most of the light came from two pool tables in back. I shuffled to the bar against the right wall, which looked to have been cobbled together from scraps of cabinet wood and countertopping, and ordered a beer. Archaeological layers of odor here: raw whiskey, stale beer, urine and sweat; the edgy smell of fish, rotting greens and sour milk from next door; under it all, mildew and mold, a fusty smell that seems to be everywhere in New Orleans.

Most of the activity, like most of the light, was concentrated around the pool tables. A man and woman barely old enough to be in here legally sat nearby at one of a number of battered, unmatched tables. The man drained his malt liquor can, reached for the woman's and said, "Now baby you *know* where I stays." There were a couple more guys at the bar perched on wobbly stilt-like stools.

"Do me a beer, man?" one of them said, turning his whole upper body to look at me. "I'm hurtin'."

He got his beer.

"Here's to Truth, Justice and the American Way," he said, lifting his glass in a toast. "All those wunful things we fought for." He belched. " 'Long with career politics, of course."

One of the players in back made a tough shot and for a while everybody kept busy walking around the tables doing high fives, slapping palms, exchanging money.

"You in here a lot?" I said.

He thought about it. "I ain't here, Luther don't bother opening up."

"Know a guy named T.C.? Regular, they tell me. Tall dude—"

He grinned. Not a good sign.

"—hair cut short, wears one earring. Light skin."

"Man, I tell you, these beers be disappearing in a hurry on a day like this one here. You notice that?"

I put another five on the bar in front of him.

"Well, then. He be coming out of the bathroom back there just about any time now, I 'spect," he said after ordering and sampling a new beer. "What you want with T.C. anyway? He ain't much."

"Friend asked me to talk to him."

"Ain't much for talk, either."

And at that, as if on cue, the man himself stepped into the penumbra of light behind the pool players, six-four or -five and at least two-fifty, all of it muscle except maybe the earring, followed a moment later by two guys in sportcoats and jeans who hurried on out of the bar.

He watched me approach without registering anything at all: alarm, suspicion, caution, interest. Or humanity, for that matter.

"Buy you a drink?" I asked.

"Why th' hell not?" And after we'd bellied up to the bar over my beer and his double Teacher's rocks, he said: "So what is it you're needing, my man? How much and when. And a name, somewhere along the way."

Faint tatters of an accent drifted to the surface, Cuban maybe.

"I'm throwing a chicken fry for my friends," I said. "Someone told me you were the man to see."

He looked at the bridge of my nose for a minute or so. No sign of alarm, suspicion, etc. (See above.)

"I get it," he said. "You're crazy, right? Like ol' Banghead Terence over there. Hey: you been buttin' down any walls lately, boy?"

"No *sir*," Terence said. My informant.

"Nigger got his head scrambled right good back there in Nam, so now every few days we'll find him in some alley somewhere and he'll be running headfirst into the wall over and over again till he falls down and can't get up no more. Wall just sits there."

He finished his drink, rolled ice around the bottom of the glass.

"Figure something like that must of happened to you. Ain't no other *possible* reason you be comin' here this way, rubbing up against me like this. You got to be crazy too. Now you tell me: am I right?''

I smiled, ordered a couple more drinks for us, and started telling him why I was there. That Sheryl wanted me to talk to him, explain why he had to leave her alone.

"So you just run on out and do whatever any pussy tell you. That it, man?''

I started over. Clare was a friend of Sheryl's and—

"So you be fucking them both at the same time? Or they do each other while you watch.''

I tried once more. I really did intend, or at least had convinced myself that I intended, just to talk to him. But intentions are slippery things.

When the gun came over the table's edge, suddenly, at the exact moment he switched his eyes toward the door and lifted his face as though in greeting, I slammed my glass down as hard as possible on that hand. The glass shattered, but I didn't feel it then. I did feel bones give way under the glass. My other hand was already moving toward him with a heavy ashtray, and that connected just above his left eye.

"Righteous," Terence said from the bar.

T.C. went back out of the chair, toppling it, but sprang almost at once to his feet and made a grab for my shirt-front. Suckered, I leaned back with the top half of my body—and he swept my feet out from under me.

"Moves," Terence said. " 'Member that shit.''

Things looked quite different from down there. It was absolutely amazing, for instance, how much bigger T.C. had gotten. Or how many cockroaches there were skittering about under chairs and things. At one point when T.C. was sitting on top of me kind of boxing my head from side to side playfully, I saw by a table leg what I'm certain was a severed, dried-up ear.

Then I watched two fingers jam up hard into his nose and heard cartilage give way there. When he lifted his hands to pull mine away, I struck him full force in the throat and he fell off me, gasping. I kicked him in the

ribs, then a couple of times in the head before I noticed
he was lying still and turning blue. No one made any
move toward us; they simply watched.

"Better call the paramedics," I told the bartender,
staggering over to him. It sounded like: *Btr. Kawl.
Thpur. Medix.*

He looked about the room, timing it.

"Man does comedy too," he said.

There was skittery laughter.

But he also said, to me: "You better get on out of
here. We'll just 'low Mr. T.C. to sleep it off a while.
But come closing I 'spect I'll notice him there. Don't
see no way 'round that. And then the Man's gonna want
to know things."

I started out.

"That be two-ninety for the last round," the bartender
said.

8

I RANG THE BELL AND THEN JUST KIND OF LEANED there against the sill to wait. I didn't know what time it was. After one, maybe closer to two. Lights still burned in many of the houses. Streetlights, moon and windows all had a red haze about them. I'd wrapped a handkerchief around my hand, but it was soaked through now, and periodically thick gobbets of blood would squeeze their way out and fall like slugs.

After a while I heard her coming to the door, duh-DA, duh-DA, duh-DA, in perfect iambs. She wore a short, sky-blue, kimonolike robe.

"Don't tell me," she said. "You wanted to beat the rest of the kids to the candied apples and other treats."

"Already been tricked," I said. Then: "You should see the other guy."

"Who won?"

"I did."

"Then I don't think I want to see the other guy. Aren't you getting a little old for this?"

"Tried to tell you that. Damn glad now I *didn't* wear my tie-dye."

"Sheryl's ex-live-in?"

"The chicken man himself."

"Oh Lew. I'm so sorry."

"Sorry enough to let me come in?"

"What? Oh, sorry. Sure. You really do look like shit, by the way." She turned and stepped away from the door. I took a step forward. Nations disappeared, new suns appeared in the sky, planets formed around them. I took another step.

"Are you okay?" she asked.

"Just a little damaged in transit, as they say at the post office. Then, of course, they hand you this thing that's taped back together three ways from Sunday and whatever was inside is crushed beyond recognition."

"Are you?"

"Crushed? Absolutely. Many times over. But it always springs back. Well, these days I guess it's more like it *seeps* back."

"Stronger than before?"

"Not that I've noticed. You?"

She shook her head. "Be nice if it were true, though. Like a lot of things."

I eased myself onto the couch.

"Tell Sheryl T.C. won't be bothering her anymore. Actually, I'm not sure he'll be bothering *anyone* anymore."

"Must have been one hell of a talk."

"*I* won't forget it soon. You got anything to drink?"

"Might be some scotch under the cabinet from when my parents were here. Want me to look?"

"Oh yes."

There were a couple of inches left in the bottle she put on the coffee table before me. Ignoring the glass, I tilted the bottle up. Seemed easier that way: less movement, less pain. I remembered O'Carolan asking for Irish whiskey on his deathbed, saying it would be a terrible thing if two such friends should part without a final, farewell kiss. I tilted the bottle again.

"I feel like I just blinked and twenty years went by—backwards," I said. "Definitely an old TV science fiction show. Can't be real life." I looked at her. "Sorry. It's late."

"It's okay, Lew. Really."

"Tell you what. I'm going into that bathroom down there at the end of the hall to face up to some hot water and soap. Pay no attention to screams, and if I'm not out in ten minutes, you can decide on your own whether to call paramedics or the funeral home. *I* sure as hell don't know which, even now."

"Need any help?"

"Me? Look at what I've already accomplished, all by myself."

"I'll make coffee, then. Once I'm up, that's usually it for the night."

I stepped carefully down the hall. Must be heavy winds and a storm coming up: the ship listed badly both to port and starboard.

Ablution accomplished, nerve ends singing like power lines in a hurricane, I came back and sat as Clare poured something yellow into the cuts, smeared on antibiotic salve and bound my hand tightly in gauze.

"That's going to need stitches. Lucky you didn't cut a tendon or an artery."

"It's not bleeding anymore. It'll be okay."

"Lew, don't you think you've worn your balls as a hat long enough for one night? Jesus!"

"Okay, okay. You're right."

"You'll go to the ER?"

"Tomorrow."

"Promise?"

I nodded and she went out to the kitchen, brought back a lacquered wooden tray with coffee in one of those thermal pitchers, two mugs, packets of sugar and sweetener, an unopened pint of Half & Half.

She poured for both of us and we sat there like some ancient married couple, sipping coffee together in the middle of the night without speaking. The moon hung full and bright in the sky outside, and after a while Clare got up and turned off the room's lights. Then, after sitting again, finishing her coffee, pouring anew for us both, she said quietly, "I don't understand what happened between us, Lew."

I said nothing, and finally she laughed. "Guess I'll put that on the list with quantum mechanics, the national debt and the meaning of life, huh?"

I looked at her.

"I'd come over there and sit at your feet now if I could, Lew. Just lean back against you and forget everything else. That's what I'd do if I could. But I can't. Probably fall, if I tried. Coffee okay? You want a sandwich or anything?"

"The coffee's wonderful, Clare. *You're* wonderful. And I'm sorry."

A silence. Then: "You have things you'd do, too—if you could?"

I nodded. Oh yes.

Another, longer silence. "Think maybe you'd consider spending the night in this wonderful coffee maker's bed?"

"I'm not in very good shape."

She laughed, suddenly, richly. "Hey, that's *my* line."

Later as we lay there with moonlight washing over us and the ceiling fan thwacking gently to and fro, I mused that pain was every bit as wayward, as slippery and inconsistent, as intentions.

"Half in love with easeful death," Clare said, striking her right side forcibly with the opposite hand and laughing. "Little did he know. But what's left is for you, sailor."

Human voices didn't wake us, and we did not drown.

9

IT WAS NOT A HUMAN VOICE AT ALL TO WHICH I woke, in fact, but a cat's. Said cat was sitting on my chest, looking disinterested, when I opened my eyes. Its own eyes were golden, with that same color somewhere deep in a coat that otherwise would have been plain tabby. *Mowr*, it said again, inflection rising: closer to a pigeon's warble than anything else.

"You didn't tell me there was a new man in your life," I said when Clare came in with coffee moments later.

"Yeah, and just like all the rest, too: only way I can keep him is to lock him in at night. Lew, meet Bat."

She put a mug of *café au lait* on the table by me and held on to the other, which I knew would be only half filled, to allay spillage.

"I was in the kitchen one morning, bleary-eyed as usual, nose in my coffee. Glasses fogging over since I hadn't put my contacts in yet. I heard a sound and looked up and there he was on the screen. Just hanging there, like a moth. I shooed him down but a minute later he jumped back up. That went on a while, till I finally just said what the hell and let him in. From the look of it, he hadn't eaten for a long time.

"He was just a kitten then. There wasn't much to him but these huge ears sticking straight up—that's how he got the name. I asked around the neighborhood, but no one knew anything. So now we're roomies. He's shy."

"I can tell." I wanted the coffee bad, but the cat didn't seem to understand that.

"No, really. I bet he spent all night behind the stove, just because he didn't know you."

"Help?" I made clawing motions toward the coffee mug.

"What? Oh sure." She scooped the cat up in an arm (it hung there limper, surely, than anything alive can possibly be) and dropped it onto the floor (where it grew suddenly solid and bounded away into the next room). "Hungry?"

"Yes, but it's my treat. What time is it, anyway?"

"Eight-thirty."

"Aren't you late?"

"I called in."

"Not feeling good, huh?"

"*Au contraire*, believe me."

"Okay. So we can make the Camellia when it opens. Before the crowd hits. If that's all right."

"That's great."

We splashed water on faces, brushed teeth (unbelievably, she still had a toothbrush of mine there), dressed (as well as clothes to replace encrusted ones from the night before), and took her car uptown. Since the car was specially outfitted, there was never any question who would drive. She parked by an elementary school on the far side of the neutral ground and we walked across Carrollton, dodging a streetcar that lugged its way toward St. Charles beneath towering palms, bell aclang. She was wearing sneakers, jeans and an old sweatshirt from the rehab hospital that read *Do It—Again.*

Lester told us how good it was to see us after so long, wiped quickly at the counter, set out tableware rolled into crisp white napkins. Without asking, he brought coffees with cream, and within minutes was also sliding our breakfasts onto the counter before us, pecan waffle for Clare, chili omelette for me.

We ate pretty much in silence, smiling a lot, then walked over to Lenny's so she could get a *New York Times*.

"What now, Lew?"

"Maybe you could drop me off at Touro's ER."

"Would you mind too much if I stayed with you? It'll probably be a long wait, and you never know how you might be feeling afterward."

"You don't have to do that, Clare."

"I know I don't."

So she did.

At the triage desk I gave my name and other information to the clerk, answered that no I had no medical insurance but would be paying by check for services rendered, and earned for that a lingering, weighty glance, as though it were now moot whether I was the worst sort of social outcast and deadbeat, or someone important who perhaps should be catered to.

"Please wait over there, Mr. Griffin," he said, pointing to row upon row of joined plastic chairs I always think of as discount-store pews. "A doctor will see you shortly."

Shortly turned out to be just under three hours.

The place was more like a bus station than anything else. That same sense of being cut off from real time, much the same squalor and spread. Everything stank of cigarette smoke, stale ash and bodies. Stains on the chairs, floor, most walls. Steady streams of people in and out. Some of them picnicking alone or in groups from fast-food bags and home-packed grocery sacks, a few to every appearance (with their belongings piled alongside) homesteaded here.

Periodically police or paramedics pushed through the automatic doors with drunks, trauma victims, vacuum-eyed young people, sexless street folk wound in layers of rags, rapists and rapees, resuscitations-in-progress, slowly cooling bodies. Every quarter hour or so a name would boom over the intercom and that person would vanish into the leviathan interior. None of them ever seemed to emerge. Nurses and other personnel strolled past regularly on their way outdoors to smoke.

A young woman from Audubon Zoo came in with the hawk she'd been feeding attached to her by the talons it had sunk into her left cheek.

A detective from Kenner arrived to inquire after a body that had been dumped on the ER ramp earlier that morning allegedly by a funeral home that claimed the next of kin refused to pay them.

An elderly woman inched her way in and across to the desk to ask please could anyone tell her if her husband had been brought here following a heart attack last night, she couldn't remember where they said they were bringing him and had tried several other hospitals already and didn't have any more money for cab fare.

Clare, it turned out, was right on several counts. Once the whale finally got around to swallowing me, I emerged with a dozen or so stitches. I emerged also, barely able to walk, on wobbly legs, demonstrably in poor condition to attempt wending my way home unaided.

To her credit, she made only one comment as she watched me wobble toward her in the waiting room: "Well, *here's* my big strong man." Then she took me home.

I woke to bleating traffic and looked at the clock on my bedside table. Four fifty-eight. From the living room I could hear, though the volume was low, Noah Adams on NPR, interviewing a man who had constructed a scale model of the solar system in his barn.

Clare sat in the wingback reading, a glass of wine beside her.

"I know it would be far, far too much to hope that, anticipating this second, unexpected morning of mine, you might have coffee waiting."

"*Fresh* coffee, as a matter of fact." She glanced at

the wall clock. Time—thief of life and all good intentions. "Well, an hour ago, anyway."

It was wonderful.

I drank the first cup almost at a gulp, poured bourbon
into the next and nursed it deliciously. We sat listening
to traffic sounds from Prytania, a block or so away, and
to an update on Somalia relief efforts.

"I ever tell you about my father?" Clare asked.

"Some. I know he died of alcoholism when you were
still pretty young. And you told me he was a champi-
onship runner in college."

"Leaves a lot of in-between, doesn't it?"

"That's what life mostly is, all the in-between stuff."

"Yeah. Yeah, I guess so." She crossed her leg and
leaned toward me, wine washing up the side of her glass
in a brief tide. "I don't remember a lot, myself. Mostly
I have these snapshots, these few moments that come
back again and again, vividly. So vividly that I recall
even the smells, or the way sun felt on my skin."

A woman walked down the middle of the street pushing a shopping cart piled with trash bags. White ones,
brown ones, black ones, gray ones. An orange one with
a jack-o'-lantern face.

"I remember once I'm sitting in his lap and he's telling me about the war. That's what he always calls it,
just 'the war.' And he says, every time: a terrible thing,
terrible. And I can smell liquor on his breath and the
sweat that's steeped into his clothes from the roofing job
he's been on all day over near Tucson.

"You know about code-talkers, Lew? Well, he was
one of them. The Japanese had managed to break just
about every code we came up with, I guess, and finally
someone had this idea to use Indians. There were about
four hundred of them before it was all done, all of them
Navajo, and they passed critical information over
the radio in their own language, substituting nat-

ural words for manmade things. Grenades were potatoes, bombs were eggs, America was *nihima*: our mother.

"They were all kids. My father had gone directly from the reservation up near Ganado into the Marines. He was seventeen or eighteen at the time. And when he came back, three years later, to Phoenix, he couldn't find work there. He wandered up into Canada—some sort of pipeline job or something, I'm not sure—and he met Mama there. The sophisticated Frenchwoman. The *Québecoise*. Who devoted the rest of her life, near as I can tell—though who can say: perhaps misery was locked inescapably into his genes—to making the rest of *his* life miserable.

"By the time he died he'd become this heavy dark bag my mother and the rest of us had to drag behind us everywhere we went. What I felt when he died, what my mother must have felt, was, first of all, an overwhelming sense of relief.

"I think about that still, from time to time. The feelings don't change, and it seems somehow important to me that I don't lose them, but it does keep flooding back. Like givens that are supposed to lead you on to a new hypothesis. . . . You have any idea at all what I'm talking about?"

"Not much."

"Neither do I. But I *almost* had it, just for a moment there."

" 'Keep trying.' "

"Tolstoy dying—right?"

"Scratched it with a finger on his sheet, yes."

"What would *you* scratch out, Lew?"

"Something from a poem I read a while back, I think: 'find beauty, try to understand, survive.' "

Moments later: "You ready for bed?"

"Hey, I just got up."

"So? What's your point?"

Mozart replaced Noah Adams, traffic sounds relented, the old house creaked and wheezed. We got up a couple of hours later and walked over to Popeye's for chicken, biscuits, red beans and rice.

10

I GOT HOME MIDMORNING AND WAS WALKING TOWARD the answering machine with its blinking light when the phone itself rang.

"Lew," Achille Boudleaux said. "You look'n 'roun' for me, I hear." He could speak perfectly proper, unaccented English if he wanted, but rarely bothered without good reason, and never among friends.

I said there was absolutely no way he could know that.

"Why I so damn good. What you wan'?"

I filled him in, including my tracking down Garces at the shelter.

"Is there anything else, A.C.? Something you may have left out of the report? However tenuous it might seem."

"Hol' on. I done pull out the notebook cause I know what you wan' me for."

Virtual silence on the line. A match striking in Metairie and a long pull on his cigarette. A cough that died aborning, rattling deep in his chest like suppressed memories. Car alarm somewhere down the street. Police siren racing up Prytania.

"Ain' much here, Lew. One t'ing I din't put in, but issa long shot, pro'ly don' lead nowhere. Miss Alouette, she bin keepin' comp'ny wit' a guy call hi'self Roach, some say. Make goo' money, that boy, but he don' seem to work at anythin', you know? He from up 'roun' Tup'lo."

58

"You have any idea how long they'd been a number?"

"Don't know they were, rilly."

"Any address for this Roach?"

"You bin off the street too long, Lew. Roaches don't have no 'dress, you know that. You wan' him, you just get on downtown and ax 'roun'. "

"Okay. *Bien merci*, Achille."

"*Rien.*"

I cradled the phone and hit *Message*. After a brief pause, a momentary shush of tape past pinions, Richard Garces identified himself, saying: "Give me a call when you can. I think I have a couple of leads on Alouette."

I dialed, got a busy signal three times in a row, at last got through and was put on hold. "You're So Vain" fluted into my defenseless ear and I found myself thinking about Carly Simon's lips. Something I was pretty sure Richard Garces never did.

"Mr. Griffin," he said. "Sorry to keep you waiting. Something of an emergency with one of my girls."

"Lew—remember? And no problem."

"Super. Okay, here's the thing. I'm a hacker, or at least I was a while back, and there was a time there when a lot of us kind of stumbled into one another over the years on various bulletin boards. We were all doing social work, that's what brought us together. Some like myself in small shelters or support services scattered throughout the country, some in institutions, most in public health—MHMR or other government services. Those early contacts developed into a loose network, a place we could go for information we didn't otherwise have access to, a kind of information underground."

"Right." The country—whatever your special interest: law, liberal politics, magazine sales, white supremacy—was rife with such networks, electronic and otherwise. Often I imagined they might represent this skewed nation's only true intelligence, skein after skein of fragile webs piling one atop another until a rudimentary nervous system came into being.

"Well, I hadn't logged on to the network in quite a while. My work here at Foucher's pretty circumscribed. But after you left the other day, after I'd thought about it a while, I got on-line. And after half an hour or so of 'Good to see your number come up' and 'How's it been going' and 'Where the hell you been, man'—I guess the economy's gotten so bad that these guys don't have much else to do but sit home, stroke and get stroked by electronic friends—I started asking about an eighteen-year-old who might give New Orleans as a prior address, might be reluctant to say more and is probably in trouble.

"That's what the network's about, after all. Alouette doesn't have any resources, any skills. Wherever she winds up, sooner or later she's going to have to hook into one of the available programs."

"And you can track her that way."

"Ordinarily, no. Well, I guess you *could*, but it would take forever. There's no official channel. No central data bank or clearinghouse. The network itself is sketchy, but we've got people scattered all through the country, at all levels, and every one of us is facing the same problems day in and day out, a lot of them basically insoluble. So sometimes we're able to help one another. Provide information or a way around this or that obstacle, maybe cut a corner or two."

Okay, so it reeked of J. Edgar Hoover-style rationalization. And sure, you had to wonder to what use those less scrupulous might put such information, were it available to them. But I had no reason to believe that Richard Garces was any less liberal in reflex or thought than myself: he'd doubtless covered this same ground many times over.

"You have any indication Alouette was pregnant?" he asked suddenly.

"Not really. Did you?"

"It's a possibility. You have a pen and paper?"

"Yeah." I always kept early drafts and aborted pages, folding them in half to make a rough tablet that stayed there by the phone.

"Okay. Out of a couple dozen maybes, I boiled it down to three. These may all be way off base, you understand. Wrong tree—even wrong forest, for all we know. But age, accent and physical description are all good matches."

"I understand."

"The first one showed up in Dallas a few months back, brought into Parkland when she was raped by some guys who were looking through the Dumpster she lived in for leftover hamburgers and found her instead. It was behind a Burger King. Right now she's in the Diagnostic Center. That's around the corner from Parkland, up on Harry Hines. She'll be there another few days, then she'll be farmed out to whatever treatment center or hospital has a bed open up. Gives her name as Delores, and says no next of kin. Right age and general physical appearance."

"Have a number for the place?"

He gave it to me and said, "I don't know how much good this will do you. Phones there tend to be answered by untrained attendants who have little comprehension of what they're up against, even less of any moral and constitutional limits to their protectorship."

I knew just what he meant, recalling sojourns in psychiatric hospitals and alcohol-treatment centers where constitutional rights, legal principle and simple human dignity were violated unthinkingly and as a matter of course.

"Second is over at Mandeville, the state hospital. Listed as Jane Doe, since all she'll say is 'God listens, the angels hear.' Her social worker's name is Fran Brown." He read off a number and extension.

"Third's up in Mississippi. This is the pregnant one.

Was pregnant, anyhow: she delivered last week. Way premature. The baby's in NICU, barely a pound. And barely hanging on, as I understand. As you'd expect. Her case worker is Miss Siler." He spelled it. "That's all I could get: Miss Siler. No first name, credentials, job title. Girl gave *her* name as McTell. No record of social dependence—as we put it—in Mississippi. No medical coverage or prenatal care, and no father of record entered."

Again, he read off a number.

"Got it. Thanks, Richard. You ever want to get into a new line of work, you'd make one hell of a detective."

"Yeah, well. Once in a while we do something that really helps, you know. I hope this is one of those times. A favor?"

"You got it."

"Let me know?"

"Absolutely."

So then I had to go find Roach, of course.

Bars, taverns, street corners. The Hummingbird Grill, the Y at Lee Circle, Please U Restaurant, a group of men seated as usual on the low wall before a parking lot. One establishment had as identification only a piece of cardboard with *Circle View Tavern* hand-lettered on it; it was taped to the window among campaign posters (*Dr. Betty Brown, School Board, Third Ward: Your Children Need Her*) and long-out-of-date showbills (*Catch Some Soul at Fat Eddie's*).

I asked at Canal and Royal, again at Carondelet and Poydras, around Jackson Square, along Decatur, Esplanade and into the Faubourg Marigny. When New Orleans's founding Creoles overflowed the Quarter, they spilled into the Marigny—years before Irish, British and other Anglo settlers began moving into the regions above Canal. When I first came to New Orleans, the Quarter itself was crumbling and everything below Esplanade was strictly no-man's-land. Then, gradually, those buildings were reclaimed; and in recent years the

Marigny's become a cozy residential area where alternative bookstores, lesbian theaters, small clubs and flea markets thrive.

One small corner bookstore there has, packed in with Baldwin, Kathy Acker, Virginia Woolf, Gore Vidal and a wall of books on sexuality, what must be the definitive collection of a genre few know exists: lesbian private-eye novels. I counted once, and there were fourteen different titles; whenever I'm in the Marigny I drop by to check for new ones. This time when I stepped in off the sidewalk a face turned up to me and its owner carefully set back on a shelf the book he'd been paging through.

"Lew," he said.

It was Richard Garces. "What are you doing here?" seemed a pretty stupid question, but I asked it anyway.

"I live here. Buy you a drink?"

"Why not?"

We walked down to Snug Harbor and settled in at a table by the window. Women in cotton dresses and army boots went by. Men with ponytails and expensive Italian suitcoats worn over ragged T-shirts and jeans. Richard and I decided on two Heinekens.

"I've been down here almost since it started," he told me. "Had a store myself for a while, sold prints and original photographs, a lot of it friends' work. Paid someone else to run it, of course. I still do a turn now and again at the Theater Marigny, and I work weekends on the AIDS hot line."

"A pillar of the community."

"*My* community, yes. Actually I am."

A middle-aged couple came in and stopped by our table to say hello to Richard before moving on to a table of their own. It was obvious from their ease with one another that they'd been together a long time. Both were black, introduced by Garces as Jonesy and Rainer (not René: he spelled it). A youngish woman came and peered into the window, hands curved around her eyes like binoculars, before stomping away. She wore a taffeta party dress, Eisenhower jacket and old high-top black basketball shoes.

"I had no idea you were gay, Lew," Richard said. "Not often I miss the call, after all these years."

"You still haven't missed it."

"Oh?"

"Oh."

"Hear that a lot."

"I bet."

"And you're not even going to tell me some of your best friends are gay?"

"No, but just between the two of us, one or two of them are black."

He laughed, and finished off his beer. "Well, I'm sorry to hear that. The first thing, I mean. And I have to tell you, there's a certain sense of loss involved here. You want another beer?"

Our waiter glided new bottles soundlessly into the shadow of former ones. Richard leaned across the table and poured anew into my glass.

"I guess you're sure about that," he said.

"For the moment, anyhow."

"So: what? You're just down here slumming? Looking for Fiesta Ware to complete your set, maybe? Soaking up local color for a new book?"

"Something like that."

"Yeah, well." He drank most of his beer at a gulp. "So now I just say good to see you and go home alone, huh?"

"Way things are."

He killed it. "Okay. That's cool." He extended his hand across the table and we shook. "Take care, Lew."

"And you."

After he was gone I asked for coffee, got something that had been sitting on the back burner since about 1964 and drank it anyway. Thinking now of many things. Walking thick woods in predawn mists beside my father, the smell of oil from his shotgun at once earthy and sharp in my nose. Vicky and I on our first, awkward dates. LaVerne twenty-six years old in a white suit across the table from me at Port of Call. My son's last postcard, and the taped silences from my answering machine that I somehow always knew were from him and still kept in a desk drawer.

Ceaselessly into the past. Kierkegaard was right: we understand our lives (to the extent that we understand them at all) only backwards.

Backwards was the way I caught up with Roach, too, as it turned out.

Like many city dwellers, I try to carry a kind of bubble of awareness around me always, alert to whatever happens within that radius. And now as I stepped off a curb, without knowing how or where, I sensed the zone had been violated—just seconds before I was seized from behind, arm at my neck, and slammed against a wall.

"Say you been asking all over for the Roach and don't no one know you."

He was close to my size and at least ten years younger. Hair cut in what these days they're calling a fade. Black T-shirt, baggy brown cargo pants, British Knight sneakers the size of tugboats. A most impressive scar along almost the full length of the arm pressed against my windpipe. One dainty ceramic earring.

"Gmmph," I said.

He patted me down quickly with the other hand. "You cool?"

I said "Gmmph" again.

"Now it's jus' too damn hot for running. I have to run after you, that's gonna make me mad."

The tugboats backed out a step or two. Air shuddered into my lungs.

"Howyou . . . findme?" I said when I could.

"Shit, man. You weren't doing any good at finding *me*, so I figured I'd best come find *you*. How many old black farts you think we see down here asking for the

Roach, anyhow? And wearing a sportcoat?''

"I'm not a cop."

"Even cops ain't stupid as that. Not most of them, anyway.''

He paused to stare at a group coming toward us. They had been looking on inquisitively, but now hurried to cross the street.

"My name's Lew Griffin. I—''

"I be damn. Lew Griffin. You don't remember me, do you? Course not. No reason you should. I was in a house down here same time as you, man, must be eight, nine years ago. People wondered about you, talked some. You roomed with a guy named Jimmie later got hisself killed. Heard you did something about that.''

I hadn't—not the way he meant, anyway—but I let it pass. Never dispute a man who thinks you're a badass.

"So how you been, man?''

"Just about every way there is to be, one time or another,'' I told him. "Right now I'm good.''

"You know it.'' He stepped back, as though suddenly noticing me crowded there against the wall. "So what you want with the Roach, Griffin? You're a drinker, as I recall—and memory's my *other* thing that always works fierce. Not behind pills and powder.''

"I'm looking for a girl named Alouette. Guidry, but I don't know she'd be using that name. You know her?''

"Might. She family?''

I shook my head. "Favor for a friend.''

"Then I know her. Did, anyway. Stone fox, the way these light women get all of a sudden they're thirteen, fourteen.''

"Alouette's eighteen.''

"You know, I found that out. Had to cut her loose, too, but that wudn't the reason. Sorry to have to do it, I tell you that.''

"What *was* the reason?''

"She carrying around some heavy shit, Griffin, you know what I mean? Now I'll do a line same as the next man, I won't hold that against no one. But Lou, you let *her* do a few lines, even get a few drinks and a toke or two in her, and it'd be like this big hairy thing had climbed out of a cage somewhere. She was doing a lot of crack there toward the end, too, and there ain't no-body don't go crazy on *that* shit.''

"When did you last see her?''

"Must be four, five months ago, at least.''

"Was she pregnant?''

"Never said so. Didn't look like it.''

"You know where she was living?''

"Not right then. She'd been staying with a friend of mine over by Constantinople. But then he had some *new* friends move in, you know? She got to talking about 'going home' along about then, I remember, and one day I said to her, 'Lou, you don't *have* a home.' She slapped me. Not real hard, and not the first time. But it was going to be the last.''

"You didn't see her again?''

"Took her to the bus station that night. She ax me to.''

"Any idea where she was going?''

"Probably wherever twenty dollars'd get her. Cause that's what I gave her.''

"Greyhound station?''

He nodded and started away.

"Hey, thanks for the help,'' I called after him. "You have a name?''

"Well,'' he said, half turning back, "I used to be Robert McTell, I guess. But I ain't no more.''

TWO DAYS LATER AT SIX IN THE MORNING, BEHIND THE
wheel of a car for the first time in at least six years, I
tooled nervously out I-10 through Metairie and onto the
elevated highway stilting over bayou and swampland,
past *Whiskey Bay, Grosse Tête*, looking at walls of tall
cypress, standing water carpeted green, pelicans aflight,
fishing boats. *This is the forest primeval*—remember?
You're definitely in the presence of something primor-
dial here, something that underlies everything we are or
presume; nor can you escape a sense of the transitory
nature of the roadway you're on, perched over these bay-
ous like Yeats's long-legged fly on the stream of time.
With emergency telephones every mile or so.

Spanish moss everywhere. Gathering it used to be
full-time employment hereabouts; before synthetics, it
was stuffing for mattresses, furniture, car seats.

I was being borne back into the past in more ways
than one. The rental car was a Mazda very close in de-
sign, color and general appearance, even after these several years, to Vicky's. (In all the wisdom of her own
twenty years the agent hedged at turning it over, balking
at my lack of a major credit card, but finally accepted a
cash deposit.) And my destination, a red umbilicus on
the map, was I-55, snaking like a trainer's car alongside
the Mississippi up past river towns like Vicksburg and
Helena, with their Confederate cemeteries, tar-paper
shacks and antebellum mansions, toward Memphis. Pure
delta South. Where the blues and I were born. Since
leaving at age sixteen, I had been back just twice.

First, though—before all this history could begin re-iterating—I was called upon to support my local police lieutenant.

The call came around midnight. I'd climbed, that night, back up out of the Marigny to Canal, tried for the streetcar at St. Charles and then at Carondelet and, encountering veritable prides of conventioneers at both locations, hoofed on up to Poydras and flagged a cab, an independent with *Jerusalem Cab* stenciled on the side and its owner's name (something with a disproportionate number of consonants) on front fenders. We miraculously avoided serial collisions as the driver filled me in on the Saints and chewed at a falafel sandwich. Car and karma held, and on half a wing and muttered prayer at last we touched down, at last I was delivered, disgorged, cast up, *chez moi*.

I put together a plate of cheese and French bread and opened a bottle of cabernet. It was Brazilian, simply wonderful, and two ninety-five a bottle from the Superstore. It was also only a matter of time before other people discovered it.

Had dinner and most of the wine by the window, sunk like Archimedes, displacing my own weight, into *L'Étranger*, life for the duration of that book, as every time I read it, a quiet, constant eureka.

Then I woke half between worlds, knowing it was the phone I heard, knowing in dreams I'd transformed it to the whine of a plane, trying to hold on, impossibly, to both realities.

I finally picked the thing up and grunted into it.

"This the fucking zoo, or what?" Walsh said on the other end.

"I didn't do it."

"Didn't do what?"

"Whatever I'm suspected of. Though I feel I have to mention that back in the good old days when you were just a little younger and a lot more interested in doing your job you actually went out and *found* the suspects and didn't just call and tell them to get their butts down to the station. Course, I guess that's one of the benefits of a reputation. Bad guys hear the phone ring, know it's you, and start writing out confessions before they even answer.''

''I told you to fuck yourself lately?'' He was slurring his words terribly. I'm a man who knows a lot about slurring words. And not a little about terrible.

''Only last week. I tried. The chiropractor thinks he'll be able to help me.''

''So what's up?''

''Well, a lot of people are sleeping, for one thing— for lack of anything better to do, you understand.''

''Hey. Lew: woke you up. Sorry.''

''No problem. But look, I've got to pee and drink something. Give me a minute, okay?''

''Want me to call back?''

''No. Once is enough. Just hang on, okay?'' A morse-like bleat on the line. ''Whoa, another call. Look. I lose you, you call me back, okay?''

That other person wanted Sears, but why at this time of night I couldn't imagine. Maybe they'd sent him the wrong size cardigan.

I went out to the kitchen and put the kettle on. Had a couple of glasses of water from the tap (glass there by the sink looked okay), then stomped upstairs to the bathroom. Listened to pipes bang and groan behind the walls on the way back down.

''You still there?''

''Yeah, I'm here.'' Throat clearing. ''You got anything else you need to do first? Run out to the corner for a paper? Go grab a burger at the King? Whack off, maybe?''

''Let me think about it. What can I do for you, in the meanwhile?''

Outside, a banana-tree leaf long ago frayed by high winds now fluttered in a gentle one in the moonlight, spilling mysterious, ever-changing shapes against the window.

"Tell you what, Lew. I came home tonight about eight, and ever since, I've been sitting here at the kitchen table with a bottle of K&B's best on the table, a pizza I picked up on the way home and now can't bear the thought of even opening up, much less eating, and my Police Special. Not the Colt. That's put away by the bed the way it always is when I get home. This's the one the department gave me, I first made detective. It stays wrapped in oilcloth in the closet, you know? But tonight I went and got it."

The French call what I felt just then a *frisson*.

This too, what was happening with Walsh, was something I knew a lot about.

"Don. What's going on, man?"

"New reports came in today. Homicides down to thirty-one for this quarter. Petty crime and misdemeanors down almost twenty percent. Surprised you hadn't heard. NOPD's doing a helluva job. You be sure and write Mayor Barthelemy and the chief and tell them, as a citizen, how much you appreciate that. They're waiting to hear from you. Operators are standing by."

I heard ice clink against a glass, a swallow, then what could have been a low sob.

"She's married this guy she met, Lew. Owns some fancy-ass sporting goods store, Florida somewhere. Pogoland. Now how the fuck'd she ever meet someone like that, what's she need with that kind of shit? But she's already moved down there with him. I finally went around to see the kids—it'd been a while and she'd been dodging me whenever I called, so I was determined, and primed for a fight—and the house was empty, doors wide open, nothing in there but some empty beer cans and paper bags and a rubber or two. So I lean on a neighbor finally and find out she moved out a couple of weeks before. Then the next day, registered mail, I get papers that this guy's putting in to adopt the kids."

Ice against glass again. Don's breath catching there at the other end. A car engine clattering outside.

"I called you because you're the only one I know who's been as fucked up as I am right now, Lew. Somehow you always get through it. And you've always been a good friend."

"No I haven't, not to anyone; we both know that. But *you* have been. Look, I'm on my way, okay? We'll talk about it."

"Yeah, what the hell. You always did talk good, Lew. You gonna want some pizza when you get here?"

"Ten minutes."

"Tinmins. Right."

My neighbor three doors down owns his own cab, a bright-green, shopworn but ever-presentable DeVille. Since it spends evenings against the curb in front of his house and rarely goes back out, I guess he does all right.

Lights were on there, and a kid about twelve answered my knock and said "Yeah."

"Your father home?"

"Yeah."

After a moment I said, "Think I might speak to him?"

"Don't see why not."

After another moment: "So: what? We're just going to wait till he has to go somewhere and notices me here in the door?"

"You some kind of smartass."

"Just asking."

"Old man don't like smartasses."

This could easily have gone on all night, but the boy's father appeared behind him, peering out. He wore baggy nylon pants, a loose zipped sweatshirt, a shower cap. I'd wondered what a kid that age was doing up this time of night, but it seemed the whole family lived counter-clockwise, as it were.

"Hi, we've never met, but I live a few houses down."

"I know who you are. Raymond, you get on about your business now."

"Who is it, honey?" came a feminine voice from deeper in the house.

"Neighbor, Cal."

"I'm sorry to bother you, but—"

He held out a hand. Muscles bunched along the forearm as we shook. "Norm Marcus. Call me Norm or Marc, whichever comes easier to you. You want to come on in, have a beer or something?"

"I'd love to, but a friend of mine just called and things don't sound so good over there. Since I don't drive I wondered if—"

"You need a ride, right?"

"I'll make it worth your while."

"Worth my while, huh?" He half turned, called into the house "Be right back, Cal" and stepped out, pulling the door shut. "It's already worth my while, Lew. Man can't help a neighbor, why's he bother living anywhere—know what I mean? Where we headed?"

I got in beside him and told him the address. He punched in a tape of Freddie King, hit the lights, and swung out toward St. Charles.

I tried to pay him when we pulled up at Don's place, but he said don't insult him. "You want me to wait?"

I thanked him again and said no, and that we had to get together for that beer soon.

"Absolutely. Or you just come on by for dinner, any night. Eat about nine, usually."

The front door was locked, but like mine Don's house is an old one whose frame and foundation have shifted time and again, and whose wood alternately swells with humidity and shrivels from heat. I pushed hard at the door and it opened.

He was still there all right, in the kitchen, head down on the table, facing away from me. An inch or so of bourbon remained in the bottle. The pizza, out of the box now, lay upside down on the floor, Police Special nearby.

I quickly checked a carotid pulse. Strong and steady.

He bobbed to the surface, without moving or opening his eyes.

"You, Lew?"

"Yeah. Let's get to bed, old friend."

"I tell you my wife was fucking Wally Gator?"

I hauled him more or less to his feet and we caromed from wall to wall down the narrow hall to his bedroom. I let him go slack by the bed, went around and pulled him fully aboard. Took off his shoes and loosened belt, trousers, tie.

I was almost to the bedroom door when he said: "Lew?"

"Here."

"You're a good man. Don't ever let anybody tell you different."

I sat there in his kitchen the rest of the night, though at this point there wasn't a lot of *rest* left, fully understanding that I wasn't a good man, had never been, probably never would be. The world outside faded slowly into being, like prints in a developing tray. And when magnolia leaves swam into focus against cottony sky, I put my thoughts aside, finished the bourbon and got coffee started. Not long after that, Don's alarm buzzed into life. I walked in with two cups of *café au lait*, looked at him, and shut the damned thing off.

12

THE DEAD WALKED AT LAST, OR MORE ACCURATELY stumbled, at nine or so, into the kitchen where it looked at the clock, looked at me, back at the clock, mumbled *shit* most unexpletively, and slumped into a chair.

I poured coffee and put it down before him. He sat looking at it, estimating his chances. Gulfs loomed up everywhere. Washington and the Delaware. Napoleon crossing to Elba. Raft of the Medusa. Immigrants headed for Ellis Island, shedding history and culture like old clothes. Boats packed with new slaves, low in the water, nosing into compounds at Point Marigny across the river from what was now downtown New Orleans.

Finally he launched a hand into that gulf. It wavered but connected, and he drank the ransomed coffee almost at a gulp.

"I talk much last night?" he said partway into a second cup.

"Some."

"Before you came over here, on the phone? Or after."

"Before, mostly."

"Then I told you about Josie."

I nodded.

"And I was thinking about doing something stupid. I really don't remember too much else."

"You weren't thinking at all: you were feeling. But yes, it did look for a while like maybe you were going to stop being stupid for good."

"Yeah, well." He looked around the room, down at

the floor. "Anyhow, the moment's passed. You eat my pizza? Stuff's great for breakfast, cold, you know."

"Sorry. It was crawling across the rug, making for the door. I had to shoot it."

He shook his head. "You're a sick man, Lew."

We finished the pot and he called in while I scrambled eggs. We ate, then sat over a second pot of coffee. Heading back to bed finally, he paused in the doorway. Looked down the hall.

"Thanks, man. I won't forget this."

"I owe you a few."

"Not anymore you don't."

I found nongeneric scotch in the pantry beside five cans of stewed tomatoes, a stack of ramen noodles and two depleted jars of peanut butter, poured some into a coffee cup webbed with fine cracks beneath the surface, and dialed Clare's number. When her machine told me what to do and beeped at me, I said:

"This is your sailor, m'am. Who'd like to buy you dinner tonight, if you're free. Garces okay? Call me."

Garces is a small Cuban restaurant, tucked away in a decaying residential area a few blocks off Carrollton, as close to a special place as Clare and I had. Family-owned and -run, it started out years back as a grocery store and serves daily specials astonishingly simple and good, including a paella you'd kill for, cooked while you wait, one hour. Paella's where jambalaya came from, word and recipe freely translated.

I walked six or eight blocks and grabbed a bus on Magazine. Got home, rummaged through mail, listened to messages. Someone I didn't know wanted me to call right away. The English Department secretary needed to speak with me at my convenience. And Clare said: "Lew, I dodged home for lunch and found your message. Wish you'd gotten to me earlier, now I've already made plans. How're the sea legs? Talk to you later."

I stretched out on the couch for a nap and thought about Don, how he'd been looking lately, his long slow fall last night, this morning. Probably the steadiest man I ever knew. But you stand there peering off the edge long enough, whoever you are, things start shifting on you. You start seeing shapes down there that change your life.

The phone had been ringing a while, I realized. In my dreams I'd turned it into a distant train whistle.

The tape clicked on just as I answered, and I stabbed more or less randomly at buttons, *Answer, Hold*, trying to stop it. Taped message and entreaties to "Wait a minute, I'm here, hang on" overlapped, waves colliding into a feedback that made the room sound strangely hollow and cavernous.

"Can a girl change her mind?" Clare said when the tape had run its course.

"Why not? Always another ship coming into port somewhere."

"Okay. So I'll cancel this other thing and see you at Garces at, what? Six be okay? Want me to pick you up?"

"I'm not sure where I'll be before then. I'll meet you there."

"Then maybe I can take you home, at least."

"Just how do you mean that, lady?"

"Hmmmm . . ."

Where I was before then, as it turned out, was right there on that couch, though I did rouse a couple of times, first to answer the door and tell a private-school girl still in uniform (white shirt, blue tie, checked skirt, black flats) that I didn't need candy or wrapping paper, later to explain to an elderly Latin man that I *liked* the grass kind of high there in my patio-size front yard.

Around five I roused more definitively, showered and shaved, and called a cab.

Clare, a Corona, salsa and chips were waiting for me. A speaker set into the ceiling over our table spooled out the news in rolling, robust Spanish. We ordered—rice and black beans, shredded meat stewed with onions and peppers, a Cuban coffee for me; nachos, empanadas and croquetas for Clare—and filled in recent blanks like the old friends we were. I told her about my lead on Alouette and said I'd be out of town for a few days. She told me that Bat had claimed squatter's rights atop the refrigerator and passed along new revelations from a course in Flemish art she was taking at Tulane.

Somewhere along in there, with half or more of my beans and rice gone, I said something about knowing we'd been kind of backing away from one another these last months, and noticed she was looking into her plate a lot.

"Lew," she said when I stopped to order another coffee, "I have no idea what the hell you're talking about. You know that? I haven't been backing away. *You* have. All I've done is just keep trying, every way I know, to keep myself from taking that necessary step or two toward you. To close the distance. When the whole time that's all in the world I wanted."

My coffee came, dark and heavy and sweet as summer nights, in its stainless-steel demitasse cup and saucer.

"*I'll* tell you how you can tell the dancer from the dance," she said. "Sooner or later the dancer always has to talk about why he's doing what he does. The dance just happens." She laughed. "Yeats: what the hell did he know, anyway? Impotent most of his life. Writing all that romantic, then all that mystical, stuff. And a child again, himself, there at the end."

I pushed beans onto my fork with a chip, doused the chip in salsa and then in chopped peppers from a tiny side dish.

"So. Guess this means you're not going to take me home, huh?"

"No," she said, eyes meeting mine. "No, it doesn't mean that at all, Lew. I don't know what it means. Maybe it doesn't mean anything. Maybe meaning doesn't have anything to do with any of this."

She folded her napkin and laid it on the table.
''Coming with?'' she said.
Oh yes.
I have been so very long at sea.

13

BEFORE THE OLD MAN FINALLY GAVE UP ON IT—
before he finally gave up on just about everything—he
used to haul me out hunting with him the first few times
he went out each season. Something was supposed to
happen out there in the woods, I guess, with just the two
of us, a father and his son, men of a different size observing these ancient rituals together, but it never did.
I'd already learned to shoot, with bottles heeled into a
hillside out behind our house, and that was the part I
was interested in. So I'd just walk alongside Dad with
my old single-shot .410 cradled in the crook of an arm
and carefully pointing to the ground as he'd taught me,
in early years daydreaming about friends and would-be
friends in the neighborhood and next weekend's get-
togethers, later about the things I'd begun discovering
in books, with the twin plumes of our breath reaching
out into the chill morning and reeling back, Dad every
so often (it seemed always a continuous action) shoul-
dering his .12-gauge, firing, and tucking dove, quail or
squirrel into the game pocket of his scratchy canvas coat.
After a couple of hours we'd stop, find a tree stump and
have coffee from his thermos, wrapping hands around
nesting plastic cups for warmth. On extremely cold days
he brought along a hand warmer the size of a whiskey
flask; you filled it with alcohol, lit the wick, slid on a
cover and felt sleeve, and it smoldered there in your
pocket. We'd pass it back and forth the way men pass
around bottles of Jim Beam at deer camp, like athletes
toasting a victory. But neither of us was an athlete. And

neither of us would know many victories in his life.

I remembered all this, something I hadn't thought of in many years, as I drove up I-55 through mile after mile of unfenced farmland stretching to the horizon, past refurbished plantations, crop duster airfields and country stores selling everything a man could need, *Gas, Food, Beer*: this long sigh of the forever postcolonial South. I pulled off for coffee at truckers' roadside stops and Mini Marts where people seemed uneasy, even now, at my presence, despite (or just as easily because of) my dark suit, chambray shirt and silk tie. Attendants at gas stations watched me closely from their glassed-in pilot-houses. When I stopped for a meal at The Finer Diner near Greenville, two state policemen, bent over roast beef specials in a booth by the door, repeatedly swiveled heads my direction, conferring.

Paranoia? You better believe it. My birthright.

In the town where I grew up, there was one main street, called Cherry in my little rubber-stamp town, Main or Sumpter or Grand in a hundred others like it. At one end of this street was a café, Nick's, where my father and I in stone darkness Saturday mornings heading out to hunt would order breakfast on paper plates through a "colored" window leading directly into the kitchen (the only time I recall anyone in the family ever eating out), and at the other, ten blocks distant, a bronze statue of a World War I soldier, rifle with bayonet at ready, which everyone called simply the Doughboy.

For a period of several months when I was thirteen or so, every Saturday night, like clockwork, someone managed—no simple task, with city hall and the police station right there on the circle—to paint the Doughboy's face and hands black with shoe polish. You'd go by every Sunday morning and see one of the black trustees from the county jail up there with a bucket and rags, scrubbing it down.

Then, just as suddenly as it had started, it stopped. Some said because the smartass nigger responsible had

graduated from high school and, good riddance, gone up
North to college. Some said because Chief Winfield and
his boys had caught him in the act and done what was
only right.

And my father, from whom I never before remember
hearing a racial complaint, this man who called the children of white men he worked for *Mistah Jim* and *Miz
Joan*, said: "Lewis, you see how it is. Here we raise his
children for him, cook for him, bring up his crops, butcher
his hogs—even fight his wars for him—and he still won't
acknowledge our existence."

We were sitting on the steps of the railroad round-
house across from Nick's eating our breakfasts one of
those lightless early mornings, maybe the last before I
stopped going along. Steam rose off eggs and grits in
the cold air; our paper plates were translucent with
grease.

"You know those Dracula movies you watch every
chance you get, Lewis? How he can never see himself
in mirrors? Well, that's you, son—that's all of us. We
trip across this earth, work and love and raise families
and fight for what we think's right, and the whole time
we're absolutely invisible. When we're gone, there's no
record we were ever even here."

For years I thought of that as the day my father began
shrinking.

Now, years later, I remember it as one time among
many that he was able momentarily to rise out of the
drudge of his own life and offer an example—to give
me sanction, as it were—that in my own something
more might be possible.

It's a terrible thing, that I could ever have forgotten
these moments, or failed to understand them.

Oddly connected in my thoughts with all this as I
Mazdaed into pure Faulknerland, *Oxford*, *Tupelo*, was a
night Clare and I met, early on in our friendship, at a
Maple Street pizzeria and went on to the Maple Leaf for
klezmer music, impossibly joyful in its minor keys, clar-

inet beseeching and shrieking, stolid bass and accordion plodding on, half East Europe's jews dying in its choruses.

Here's what I think in higher flights of fancy. Once there existed beings, a race, a species (call it what you will) who truly belonged to this world. Then at some point, for whatever reason, they moved on, and *we* moved into their places. We go on trying to occupy those places, day after endless day. But we'll always remain strangers here, all of us. And for all our efforts, whatever dissimulations we attempt, we'll never quite fit.

14

LIGHTS CAME UP BEHIND ME NOT TOO FAR OUTSIDE Greenville—for all I know, the two young men who'd been enjoying their roast beef specials at The Finer Diner.

They, the lights, winked into being far back in my mirror, pinned in the distance at first, believably neons or traffic lights, or one of those blinking roadside barriers. But then they rushed in to close the gap, like something falling out of the sky, and suddenly were there behind me, filling mirror and road.

I pulled over and watched the one in shotgun position climb out and make his careful, by-the-book way toward me. Once years ago I'd made the mistake of stepping out of my car to meet a state policeman halfway and found myself suddenly face-down on the asphalt shoulder with a knee in my back. So now I sat very still, not even reaching for my wallet, watching him come toward me in the rearview, walk out of it, reappear in the wing mirror, then at the window.

He had to be midtwenties at least but looked all of sixteen, with a close-trimmed mustache, discount-store mirror shades, black goat-ropers. Coming abreast and bending down, he removed the glasses in a quick left-to-right sweep, releasing startling green eyes.

"License and registration, sir? Proof of insurance?"

I probably imagined the slight pause and emphasis on *sir*.

I reached slowly into the glove compartment for the car's papers, handed him those (in a leatherette wallet) along with my license and rental agreement. He studied them all carefully, looking from the picture on my license up to me and down again. Walked behind the car to check plates against the numbers listed.

"Would you excuse me for a moment, Mr. Griffin?"

He went back to the squad and passed documents across the sill. Waited. Exchanged a few words, straightened, came back toward me: rearview, side mirror, window.

"We apologize for holding you up, sir. You know a Lieutenant Walsh? NOPD?"

I nodded.

"He says thanks. Called headquarters here and asked us to stop you and tell you that. Said you'd be coming through in a Sears rental, gave us the plate number. Said just to tell you thanks, he wouldn't forget it—you'd know what he meant."

I smiled. Years ago when things were at their worst, Don was the one who stuck by me. First he, then Vicky, had made it possible for me to go on, helped me find long-lost Lew in brambles of remorse and inaction.

And Verne. How much of what I've become owes to Verne? I was never able to tell her what she meant to me; never really knew, until it was too late. And yet, somehow in all those years we circled and closed on one another like binary stars, all those departures and partial returns, somehow, in some indefinable manner, we had held one another up, had been able to climb together (even when apart) out of the wastes of our pasts.

How could I not have known that?

"Mr. Griffin?"

"Sorry. A sudden attack of memory."

"Right." He looked at me curiously. "Lieutenant Walsh also said we were to tell you to call if you need him. For anything, he said—anything at all."

I nodded, thanked him again.

"Drive safely, Mr. Griffin."

He tipped a brief salute against his hat brim and headed back to his squad.

An hour and spare change later I stood in my newly rented cabin at the Magnolia Branch Motel drinking the cream of a newly cracked fifth of Teacher's from one of those squat tumblers you never see anywhere else. I'd even had to unwrap the glass, like a Christmas gift, from crinkly, twisted paper. There was a strip of paper across the toilet seat. Rubber flower appliqués on the floor of the tub. The bed was equipped with Magic Fingers, but two quarters didn't persuade them to do anything.

Missagoula, Mississippi, was like a hundred other towns scattered through the South. The interstate zipped by only a few miles away but may as well have been in China. Remnants of an old town square hosted two gas stations (one of which doubled as post office), a café and steakhouse, a combined town library and meeting hall, a doughnut shop, a junk store or two, and an insurance office. For two or three blocks around that hub there were a scatter of paint and hardware stores, utility companies, used-clothing or -furniture shops. Then everything opened back up to farmland, trees and sky. I'd counted four churches, so far.

The Magnolia Branch squatted at the border of town and not-town. I can't imagine who would ever stay there, in a town like that, but rates were cheap and rooms immaculate. They still weren't very used to having blacks drop in, I'd guess. My request for a room occasioned considerable discussion behind the wall before the clerk (and owner, as I'd later discover) returned to push across a key and take two nights in advance. I asked about the possibility of getting a drink and was told I could get beer down at the café but if I wanted anything else I'd have to go over to Nathan's.

Nathan's turned out to be the gas station that didn't double as post office. I dropped off luggage at cabin six, walked back into town and, saying I understood liquor was for sale here, got ushered into a shed out back of the station. Bottles were set out on cheap steel shelving before which the attendant hovered impatiently. I pointed to the Teacher's and paid him. He followed me out, locked the door carefully behind us.

So now I stood there in my Magnolia Branch Motel doorway lapping at the first few most welcome sips of scotch and looking away (Dixieland!) into dusty Delta distances. News unrolled on the TV behind me. A coup attempt somewhere in Latin America, Philadelphia man's citizen's award revoked when it was discovered the recipient routinely molested the adolescents his Care House harbored, Housing Authority of New Orleans under investigation by feds.

Immediately upon returning to the motel I'd phoned Clare. Her recording had come on, and I'd started telling her where I was, how she could reach me. I'd got as far as the Missagoula part when she picked up.

"I'm here, Lew. *Where* did you say you were?"

I spelled it for her. I may even have got it right.

"And the girl's supposed to be there?"

"She gave it as an address at the hospital, finally, Richard said. Claimed she lived here with a relative. I'm pulling out in just a minute to try and find the place."

"Good luck, then."

"Thanks. I'll call again tomorrow."

"Lucky, lucky me!"

I finished my drink, rinsed the glass and put it face-down on a towel. I'd just pulled the door shut behind me when the phone started ringing. I unlocked the door and went back in.

"Lew," Clare said, "remember when you said that about another man?"

"What?"

"You were talking about my cat. Joking that there was a new man in my life."

"Oh, right."

"Well, there is."

"There is what?"

"A new man in my life."

I didn't say anything, and after a while she said, "You there, Lew?"

"I'm here."

"I didn't know how to tell you. I kept waiting for the right time, and it never came. Then you left, and the more I thought about it, the worse I felt. After I hung up just now, I knew I had to tell you, that I couldn't wait anymore."

"It's all right, Clare."

"It wouldn't matter if I didn't really care about you. I do, you know. I don't know what's going to happen, but I know I don't want to lose you."

We both fell silent, listening together to choruses of ghostlike voices far back in the wires, at the very edge of intelligibility.

"Oh Lew, are we going to be able to do this?"

"We've both been through a lot worse."

"Indeed we have, sailor. Indeed we have."

Silent again for a moment, we listened, but the voices, too, now were silent. Listening to *us*, perhaps.

"You'll call and let me know how it's going?"

"I will." Though as it turned out, I didn't.

"Bye, Lew. Love you."

And she was gone.

15

I STOPPED AT NATHAN'S TO ASK DIRECTIONS AND, FOL-
lowing a consultation between the surly black man
chewing on cold pizza behind the counter and a me-
chanic with grease worked into the lines of his face so
profoundly that it looked like some primitive mask,
headed out of town away from the interstate, leaving
pavement behind after a few miles, tires clawing for safe
ground among gullylike ruts, the little Mazda sashaying
and hip-heavy.

Houses were infrequent and set back off the road, simple wood structures built a foot or two off the ground,
most of them long unpainted and patched with odd
scraps of lumber, corrugated tin, tar paper, heavy cardboard. Many had cluttered front porches and neatly laid-
out vegetable gardens alongside. Small stands of trees
surrounded house and yard; beyond that, flat farmland
unrolled to every side.

I pulled in, as I'd been told back at Nathan's, by a
yellowish house on the right, first one I came to after
crossing railroad tracks and going through two cross-
roads. An old woman in a faded sundress scattered grain
for chickens at the side of the house. She was oddly
colorless, pulpy like wood long left outdoors, collapsing
into herself with the years. She looked at me with all
the interest a tree stump might display.

"Hello, m'am. Sorry to bother you, but I'm looking
for Alouette."

Nothing showed on her face. "Not bothering me,"
she said. Then she turned and walked away, to a rough

shed nailed onto the back of the house at one end, open at the other. I followed a few steps behind. She dumped grain back into a burlap bag and folded the top over. Hung the pail from a nail just above.

"Could you tell me if she's around?"

"Have to ask what your business with her might be."

"I promised a friend I'd look her up."

She grunted. It was more like the creak of a gate than any grunt I'd ever heard. "Name's Adams. Where you from, boy?"

"New Orleans."

"Mmm. Thought so." She looked to see how the chickens were doing. They seemed more interested in pecking one another than the food. "I was up to Memphis once. You been there?"

"Yes m'am, I have." Memphis was where my father died, though I wasn't there then.

"You care much for it?"

"Not particularly. It's like just about any other town you see around here, only a lot bigger."

She groaned—it couldn't have been a laugh—and said that was God's truth. Then she looked at me for a while before saying: "Well then, I guess I know who you must be. That Griffin fellow LaVerne took up with. Don't much like you, from what I know. Don't expect me to."

"You knew LaVerne, then?"

Again that long, affectless regard.

"Mother gen'rally knows her only daughter."

"I'm sorry, Mrs. Adams," I said shortly. "I didn't know. I had no idea Verne's parents were still alive."

"Just the one. But neither did she, boy, that you'd notice. Not that her daddy and I ever wanted things any different, you understand. Vernie had her life down there in New Orleans, and she was welcome to it, but *we* didn't want any part of it. Wrote once or twice."

"LaVerne really turned things around, later on. She helped a lot of other people get their lives together, too.

You both could have put all that behind you.''

''Maybe we could have. Maybe not.'' She eyed the chickens again, looked up at the sky. Darkness had begun working its way in at day's edge. ''Things had changed here too.''

''So Alouette came here because you're her grandmother?''

''You have the kind of troubles that girl had, you just naturally go to a woman. From what I know about down there where you-all are, there wasn't much of anybody she *could* go to.''

''Her mother was trying to get in touch with her, before she died. That's why I'm here now.''

''Girl didn't know that. Didn't say much about her mother ever: Not that I cared to listen.''

''How did Alouette find you here? Or even know about you, for that matter?''

''Long time ago, right after Vernie had her, I sent that girl a book of stories I came across in the back of a cabinet, something that was Vernie's when she was little. Thought she might make some use of it. Envelope had the address, and she says her mother cut that out and pasted it in the front of the book. Never sent another thing to that girl. But I ain't moved, of course. And she still had it.''

''Where's Alouette now, Mrs. Adams?''

''Couldn't tell you that, I'm afraid.''

''But she is here? With you?''

Her eyes were as lifeless as locust husks abandoned on a tree. ''Stayed here a few days. Then when it looked to be some trouble, I had Mr. Simpson drive that girl over to the Clarksville hospital. I did midwifing back in the old times. You don't forget what birthing trouble looks like.''

''Did you visit her at the hospital? Did anyone?''

''Haven't seen her since the day Mr. Simpson came by to get her.''

"Didn't you wonder how she was doing? Think she might need you?"

"Don't waste much time worrying and thinking. I figure the girl found me once. If she wants to, she can do it again. She'd be welcome enough."

"You know about her baby?"

"Mr. Simpson told me it's still alive."

"Mrs. Adams, I have to ask you something. Please don't take this wrong. Was your granddaughter using drugs when she was here?"

She thought for a moment. "Wouldn't know how to tell you. She wasn't normal. Laid around half asleep most of the time, didn't have any appetite. All that could be what was going wrong inside her."

"You don't have any idea where she might have gone, then, after leaving the hospital?"

"Didn't know she left."

"Well, I'll be getting on, then. Thank you for giving me so much of your time."

"Didn't give it. You helped yourself."

"You're right, but thanks all the same. When I find Alouette, I'll be sure to let you know."

I started back around the house to the car.

"Boy?"

"Yes, m'am?"

"You be heading over to Clarksville now by any chance?"

"Yes, m'am."

"Going to see that baby."

"Yes, m'am. And to ask more questions."

"You figure you might have room to give an old lady a ride over there? Sounds like that baby's going to be needing someone."

"Yes, m'am. It does sound that way. And I'd be glad to take you."

"You wait right there."

She went into the house and came immediately back

out with a Sunday-best purse, probably the only one she had. It was covered with tiny red, blue and green beads.

"Let's go, boy," she said. "Dark's coming on fast."

It always is.

So, MIDNIGHT, RAINING, MILES TO GO, I ARRIVED AT the berth bearing Baby Girl McTell to whatever ports awaited her.

In the car on the way Mrs. Adams asked me to tell her about Verne's last years, offering no comment when I was through. We passed the remainder of the trip, just over an hour, in silence, watching the storm build: a certain heaviness at the horizon, rumbles of thunder in unseen bellies of clouds, lightning crouched and stuttering behind the dark pane.

Mrs. Adams had me drop her off on the highway outside town, at a cinderblock church (*Zion Redemption Baptist*) where, she said, her sister lived, adding "pastor's wife," her toneless voice (it seemed to me) implying equally scorn and acknowledgment of status. She would go on to the hospital first thing in the morning.

Closer in, I stopped at one of those gargantuan installations that look like battleships and seem to carry everything from gas and drinks and snacks to novelty T-shirts, athletic shoes and the occasional Thanksgiving turkey. You could probably pick up a TV or computer system at some of these places. I pushed a dollar over the counter toward a teenage girl wearing a truly impressive quantity of denim—shirt, pants, boots, jacket, even earrings—and poured my own coffee from a carafe squatting on the hot plate (*One Refill Only, Please*) beside display cards of Slim Jims, snuff and lip balm. Then I pulled the car to the edge of the lot and sat there breathing in the coffee's dark, earthy smell, feeling its heat and steam on my face, sipping at it from time to time. New Orleans coffee makes most others seem generic, but I was at this moment far, far from home, a wanderer, and could make do. Besides, for the true believer coffee's a lot like what Woody Allen says about sex: the worst he ever had was wonderful.

Back at the hospital years ago, later at AA meetings, coffee would disappear by the gallon, as though it were getting poured down floor drains. These people were *serious* coffee drinkers. Someone or another was pretty much always at work making a new pot, draining the urn to re-up it, dumping out filters the size of automobile carburetors or measuring out dark-roast-with-chicory by the half pound. Antlike streams of porters to back doors, fifty-pound sacks saddling their shoulders. They should have just pulled up tanker trucks outside, run a hose in.

So the mind, weary from the day's travel, released for a time even from purposeful activity, wanders.

To a dayroom where a youngish man sits staring fixedly at reruns of *Hazel, Maverick, I Dream of Jeannie, Jeopardy*, swathed in the dead, false calm of drugs, mind all the while sparking and phosphorescing like the screen's own invisible dots.

To a still younger man waking against a heap of garbage bins, loose trash, half a burned-out mattress, on a New Orleans street, shotgun houses hardly wider than their entry doors in dominolike rows as far as he can see looking up from the pavement there, wondering how last night bled over into this bleary, pain-filled morning, how he shipwrecked here, wherever here is, finding what little money he had left, of course, gone.

To a teenage boy then, spine bent in a question mark above Baldwin or *Notes from the Underground* as flies buzz the screen and morning nibbles dark away from the window, a boy just beginning to sense with fear and elation how very large the world is and to believe that, turning these pages, naming things in these mirrors, he'll discover secret doors and passageways few other of the castle's inhabitants suspect.

Forward suddenly to a man in his forties as he sits over a drink and the final pages, proofing them, of a novel titled *The Old Man,* wondering if he'll ever be able to do what he has just, amazingly, done, to create so vivid and reflective a world, ever again.

Two young black men pulled in by one of the pumps. They were driving a Ford that looked as though it had been badly burned then skin-grafted with pot metal; a plywood wall of speakers replaced the backseat. Even at that remove the heavy bass, all I could really make out, tugged hard at my viscera. I swallowed the last mouthful of cold coffee, started the engine, and pulled back out onto the highway. A mile or so further along, a sign reading *Clarksville* pointed off to the right. I turned onto a two-way highway surprisingly populous with late-model cars, pickups, and several awkward, unwieldy pieces of farm machinery, like dinosaurs strayed from their own slow time, confused and lost in the furious rush of modern life.

The hospital sat on what passed for a hill in this part of Mississippi, on the far side of a city whose business district comprised maybe ten square blocks, a preponderance of its commercial space appearing to be given over to wholesale food concerns, beauty supplies and autoparts shops. *Clarksville Regional Hospital.* An automatic ticket dispenser stood sentry at the parking lot, but the gate was up. I drove in, parked and started for the building just as the rain let go.

Even inside, in the lobby, I could hear it slamming down. Windows ran with water, closing off the outer world, and when lights blinked briefly off and back on I had the momentary, terrifying sensation of being enclosed in an aquarium. I reached out and touched the wall to steady myself.

"You all right, sir?"

A young man stepped through one of the doors, two

older women close behind. They were all black, all in whites and carrying coats.

"If you're looking for the emergency room, it's down this hallway to your right. I can call help if you'd like. Or I'll walk you down myself, since it doesn't look like I'll be going anywhere soon."

I told him I was fine, just tired, that I'd been driving all day from New Orleans. Other personnel began gathering out of various hallways and doors, looking out at the downpour with irritation and anger. But even as they watched, the rain abated, settled into a soothing, slow rhythm. Most sprinted toward cars, coats or newspapers held over their heads. I asked the young man to direct me to the newborn intensive-care unit.

Then, following his instructions, I took a nearby elevator to the second floor to meet Baby Girl McTell.

FOR A LONG TIME, MEANING THAT I RARELY WOKE without memory of the previous night's events, and never in hospitals or jails anymore, I'd had my drinking under control.

I knew it wasn't that simple, of course. What is?

One of the distinctions of this addiction, because only true alcoholics have them, are blackouts. We go on moving through the physical world, driving cars, carrying on conversations and cooking meals, with whole banks of relays and higher functions closed down, unwitting passengers in our own bodies.

I was by this time a veritable quagmire of information on addiction. I could draw you diagrams, cite percentages, talk to you about noradrenaline and dopamine and receptor sites. I knew the alcoholic's body for some reason doesn't metabolize intoxicants the same way other people's do. That the addiction lodges itself where reality curves gently away from appearance, and thrives there, pushing them ever further apart. That all his life, whatever he does, a physical, psychological, ontological dialogue will be going on inside the alcoholic, and that as long as he continues to drink, however controlled it appears, sooner or later, a day, ten years, or twenty, he'll wake up once again with the world quivering terribly behind the thinnest of membranes, thoughts bending slowly, unstoppably away from one another in the terrible gravity of alcohol's black sun.

The membrane was there for me when I woke the

next afternoon. As though I were almost, but not quite, within the world; almost, but not quite, real. And as though the slightest misstep, the slightest tear at the membrane, might bring the waters of some endless night crashing down upon me from the other side.

Starting off for food after leaving the hospital, I'd changed my mind on the way and instead driven back to Missagoula, to my room at the Magnolia Branch and the Teacher's. I remembered switching on the TV, part of a talk show, a *Columbo* rerun, and a movie about aliens (it's possible that I don't have this quite right) who had learned to survive and indeed flourish by disguising themselves as Coke machines. Obviously I'd drunk the entire bottle in short order. I didn't want to think too much about what else I might have done. There was a crumpled bag in the trash, and remnants of some kind of sandwich under that, so at some point I'd gone out for food, I had no idea where.

Using what volition I had left, I showered and shaved, dressed, straightened the room, carried bags to the car and went to the office to check out. I stopped for breakfast on the highway, biscuits and gravy and lots of coffee, then drove back into Clarksville and took a room at Dee's-Lux Inn. Pale pine furniture and kidney-shaped tables from older days when motels were tourist courts and their neon signs advertised *Climate Controlled*.

I unloaded my suitcase into the top drawer of the low bureau, set my Dopp case out by the sink, and over the following days my routine varied little. I was in and out of NICU constantly, but went mostly at night, after Mrs. Adams, who kept vigil all day, sitting stiff-backed at bedside, departed, and while the British nurse, Teresa Hunt, was on duty. When I wasn't at the hospital, or trying to catch a few hours' sleep, I was scrambling after leads on Alouette.

I learned the monitors, what they were for and their various sounds; learned about blood gases and hematocrits, interstitial edemas, fibrosis, fluid overload, lipids and hyperalimentation, surfactant. I got to know several of the nurses and doctors by name, and never missed the fatigue and sadness in their eyes as they answered my questions or told me that all was pretty much as before. I spent hour after hour sitting on metal stools or in rocking chairs by Baby Girl McTell's incubator, staring in at her and speaking softly (once, not knowing what else to say, I recited "The Raven" and much of the prologue to *The Canterbury Tales*), helping Teresa or other nurses whenever I could with small tasks of caring for her.

On the streets by contrast, as I asked after Alouette, shooting pool with young hawks in satiny sweats, going into busy barbershops and sitting there as if waiting my turn for a cut while I talked to others, handing out cigarettes to elderly men clustered in scrubby street-side parks or around bars and convenience stores, I learned nothing.

Teresa and I had dinner a couple of nights, collecting surreptitious looks and the occasional outright glare at Denny's and a barbeque place, then one morning as we were leaving the hospital together, to no one's particular surprise, I think, went on to breakfast and to her house on Biscoe Street. It never happened again; there was never much question it would, really; and Teresa and I remained close.

Hospital records, as I anticipated, were of no help at all. None of the usual places a footloose young woman might alight briefly—shelters, Clarksville's only (church-run) soup kitchen, a strip of music clubs near the heart of the city—bore any visible trace of Alouette's passage. I showed her picture at malls, game arcades, on streets around what passed here for pricey downtown hotels, always prime panhandling territory.

Finally, after a couple of calls had passed back and forth between Don and myself, I met a Sergeant Travis for coffee and had him fill me in on local drug action. Much of it, he said, took place around schools and downtown bars; nothing new there. And a lot of it was small potatoes, ten or twelve hopheads carting pills, grass and cocaine, scrambling to pay for their own monkey.

I asked him about crack.

That too, he said, though it wasn't near as big here as in larger cities. Not yet, anyway.

And once you got past those ten or twelve user-friendlies?

He waited till the waitress poured more coffee and moved away. "You do not realize this is an ongoing investigation?"

"I'm not a cop or a fed. I won't step on anyone's toes. Or on my own dick."

"Yeah, well. I'm only here as a favor to NOPD. We really don't know *what* you are."

So, briefly, I told him.

He sat quietly a moment, afterwards.

"Guy calls himself Camaro's probably the one you'd want to see."

"I need to guess what he drives?"

"Prob'ly not. Around here, if he didn't sell it, he knows who did. Got tentacles running out everywhere."

"Everywhere, huh."

"I won't lie to you: there's been a couple times we were able to do one another a favor. More than a couple. You know how it is."

"You get a bust, he gets the competition offed."

"That old sweet song."

"Where's Camaro likely to be this time of day?"

"He's not at the Chick'n Shack up on Jefferson, then he's at the Broadway, a bar—and grill, the sign says, though I never saw anybody ever cook, or for that matter eat anything there—corner of Lee and Twelfth.''

"Can I say you sent me?''

"You can say whatever you want. He's only going to hear what he wants to, regardless.''

I stood and thanked him, shook hands.

"No problem,'' he told me. "May want to call in the favor someday, who knows?''

I found the eponymous pusher sitting at a booth in the Broadway, near a front window where he could keep an eye on his chariot. It was truly a splendid vehicle, beetle green with strips of chrome highlighting windows, doors, hood and trunk. A filigree of silver paint running down each side. His, their, name in silver script at one edge of the front left fender.

Camaro wore a beige suit, mostly cotton from the look of it, with a blue shirt and rust-colored tie tugged loose at the neck. The clothes set off the deep coffee color of his skin. As he lifted his drink, I caught a glimpse of gold watch and signet ring. He looked for all the world like a successful C.P.A. decompressing after a day at the computer.

He watched me walk over and sit across from him in the booth. The waitress was there instantly, dropping one of those stiff little napkins on the table in front of me. I ordered a scotch, water by. Sat drinking it, smiling over at him.

"Hope I ain't bothering you too much, sitting here like this,'' he said after a while.

I shook my head, smiled some more.

"I mean, you got friends or the rest of your band coming or something, you just let me know and I'll be glad to make room, okay?''

He took a long pull off his drink, pretty much killing it. Held up a hand to signal the waitress.

"You about ready for another one, too, friend?''

I laid a ten on the table. "My round.''

"Whatever you say.''

I introduced myself and over that drink and another, we talked as freely as two black men with secrets, rank strangers to one another, ever can. Camaro's mind was orderly and sharp; his world was a kind of pool or glade where the edges of discrete bodies of information glided by one another, sometimes catching. When I told him about Baby Girl McTell, he said he'd had a kid years ago, when he wasn't much more than one himself, that it had lived three weeks in an incubator, shriveling up the whole time till it looked like a piece of dried fruit, and then died.

I said I was looking for the baby's mother. Explained that she'd left the hospital and not gone back to her grandmother's, had dropped out of sight.

"And she's a user," he said, at my sudden glance adding: "Only reason you'd be here. That what messed the baby up?"

I nodded.

"Shit does that. People ought to know it. Course, people ought to know a lot of things." He held up his glass, looked through its amber to the light outside. I knew from long experience just how that warms the world and softens it. "You want another one?"

"Better not. Still a lot to do. We square with the tab?"

"It's cool." He looked at his watch. "Well, I've got an appointment myself. Tell you what." He slid out of the booth and stood. Bent to pick up, yes, a briefcase. "I'll ask around, see what I can come up with. You have a picture of this girl?"

I took out my wallet and gave him one of the copies. Also one of my cards, scribbling the motel's phone number on the back, then, after a second's thought, the NICU number and *Teresa*.

"If you can't get me, leave a message for her. And thanks, man."

He shrugged. I sat and watched as he climbed into the Camaro, buckled up, started the engine, hit his turn signal and eased out into traffic, sunlight lancing off the chrome.

18

My second week in Clarksville, on a Tuesday, I got back to the motel midmorning, having left the hospital at five or so and been on the streets since (with a stopover at Mama's Homestyle for a kickass breakfast), and found two messages waiting. I didn't look at the second one till later. But Teresa had called to say they were "having some trouble" with Baby Girl McTell and she thought I might want to be there.

A nurse I hadn't met before, Kristi Scarborough, brought me up to date. Around six that morning, stats had dropped into the seventies and hovered there; ABG's confirmed a low PO_2 and steadily increasing PCO_2. It could, of course, be a number of things: cardiac problems, a sign that the lungs were stiffening beyond our capacity to inflate them, infection, pulmonary edema. The baby was back on 100 percent oxygen, and ventilator pressures had been raised. Gases were slowly improving. I stood before an X-ray viewer staring at loops of white in Baby Girl McTell's belly. Like those ancient maps where the round, unknown world has been cleft in half and laid out flat. Necrosis of the bowel, Nurse Scarborough told me; a further complication. It almost always happens with these tiny ones. But for now she's holding her own.

Kristi used to work the unit full-time, she told me, but last year had married one of the residents and now put in only the hours necessary to keep her license, a day or two every other week, while husband John oversaw an emergency room just across the Tennessee line, broken bones, agricultural accidents and trauma from the regional penitentiary mostly (once, a hatchet buried in a head), and "they" tried as best they could to "get pregnant."

I left at three or four, finally, once Baby Girl McTell seemed to be out of immediate danger, and over a cheeseburger and fries at Mama's looked at the second message.

Call me. Clare.

I went back to my room and did just that. She answered on the third ring, breathing hard.

"Greetings from the great state of Mississippi."

"Lew! I've been worried about you."

I told her about Baby Girl McTell.

"Hospitals are tough. You haven't found Alouette yet, I take it?"

"She's as gone as gone gets. But I will."

"I know. I've missed you, Lew. Any idea when you'll be back in town?"

"Not really. I don't know what I'm into here, or how long it may take. I'll give you a call."

Outside, a fire truck and police car went screaming by.

"I spent about half of my teenage years waiting for people to call who said they would, Lew."

"I'm sorry," I said after a moment.

"I know. You really are—that's what makes it so difficult." I listened to the sirens fade. Wondered if she could hear them, all those miles away. "But it *is* good to hear your voice."

The door slammed in the room next to mine and a woman stalked toward her car, a pearl-gray Tempo. She got in and started it, then sat there with the engine running. A man came out of the room and leaned down to the window, holding his hands palm up.

"You're very important to me, Clare."

"I know, Lew. I know I am."

The man walked around the car and got in. They drove away.

"When I get back—if it's possible, and if you want to, that is—I'd like for us to spend some time together. A lot of time."

She was silent a moment, then said, "I'd like that too, Lew."

"Good. I guess I'd better try to get some sleep now."

"Take care."

I hung up and watched my neighbors pull the Tempo back into its slot, get out together and go back into their room.

An hour later I got up and, sitting naked on the side of the bed, improvising abbreviations in my rush to get it all down, scribbled ten pages of notes.

In a featureless gray room with light slanting in through windows set high in the wall a man says good-bye to a group of men we slowly realize are his fellow prisoners, the community he's lived among for almost ten years. He is being released because another man has confessed to the murder for which he was convicted, and which he in fact committed. He distributes his few possessions: half a carton of cigarettes, a transistor radio, a badly pilled cardigan. No one says much of anything. He turns and walks to the door, where a guard joins him to escort him out. "Don't do nothing I wouldn't do," Bad Billy says behind him, but he can't imagine anything Bad Billy would not do—or hasn't done, for that matter. He will go out into the world and find that he is absolutely alone and hopelessly unsuited for the narrow life available to him. And so he will invent a life, a thing that makes a virtue of his apartness, cobbled together from routine, false memories, old movies, half-read books. Until one day a woman will come suddenly, un-expectedly ("like a nail into cork") into his life's ellip-sis to disrupt it; and, as he struggles up out of his aloneness, as he fights against his own instincts and the circumstances of his life just to make this single human connection, his careful, wrought life collapses. When he steps out into sunlight now, it blinds him.

Those ten pages, virtually word for word as I scribbled them in the motel room that night, became the first chapter, and the very heart, of *Mole*, a book unlike anything else I had written, purely fiction in that every character, every scene was invented, purely true in that it is in purest form the story of all our lives.

19

THE DESK CLERK AND I OBVIOUSLY WERE NOT DESTINED to become close friends. He wasn't accustomed to taking messages for guests and didn't like it much, and as I came in from the hospital the next morning, he motioned at me through the front glass (a hand held high, opening and closing twice, as though waving good-bye to himself) then wordlessly shoved a couple of slips of paper over to me.

Of course, one had to take into account that he seemed to work around the clock—whenever my erratic *va et vient* took me by the office, day or night, I'd look in and see him here—which is enough to make even one of Rilke's angels growl.

Teresa had called to let me know that, minutes after I left the unit that morning, someone had tried to reach me. I flipped over to the second slip of paper, which just read *Camaro*, then back to the first. *Said you might want to check out a house in Moon Point. No direct connection that he knows, but things happen there. Hope this makes sense to you, Lew.* And an address, of sorts.

They grow their boys tough out there by the catfish channels, I want you to know, and they ain't *about* to bend over for no big-city dude in a coat and tie.

I always forget how very much alike rural and inner-city attitudes are.

Asking at the motel office, a gas station nearby, another on the highway and, finally, a postman I drove by a couple of times on a dirt road six or eight miles outside Clarksville, I found the house, a two-story frame, white many years ago. A jeep and a '55 Chevy rusted away on blocks in the front yard. There were some appliances, including a vintage avocado refrigerator, sitting at precarious angles at the side of the house. A tractor covered in vines at the back. Two Mustangs and a BMW in the circular front drive.

I knocked at the door and politely inquired after Alouette to the young man in the beige silk suit and black T-shirt who eventually answered. A relative, I told him.

"Ain't here," he said after a moment.

"Thank you. But allow me to make an assumption, possibly unwarranted, from that. To wit: that she has, at some unspecified point in the past, been here, though she is not presently."

"Say what?"

Another youngish man, unseen, joined him at the door: "What's up, Clutch?"

"Nigger looking for his squeeze."

"Yeah? He think we run some kind of dating service here? Tell him to get missing."

"You heard the man," Silky said.

"What man? All I heard's your boy hiding back there behind the door."

Silky sighed, and said door flew open. I have to tell you he was one ugly black man. Someone had been really creative with a knife or razor down both sides of his face and in one long jagged pull across his neck. The nose had spent as much time taped as not. He would have struck terror in all hearts, save for his stature: he was well under five feet tall. His body looked to be normal size, but everything else seemed oddly foreshortened. Neck, arms, legs, fingers. Temper.

"*I* got your assumption, motherfucker. Right here."

"Excuse me," I said, looking straight ahead, "I hear something, but I don't see anyone."

Which was how I got the shit beat out of me again. Or how it started, anyway. I'd never make it as a standup comic, I guess.

The first guy went low, tumbling me over, as his dwarfish buddy scrambled up my back like a chimp and started hammering temples and kicking kidneys with considerable fervor. The taller one was trying valiantly to get a knee into my groin. I reached down and grabbed his nuts, crushing them together in my fist, bringing him up off the floor like an epileptic.

At the same time, holding on, I reached out and snagged in my left hand a thick wedge of wood used in warmer days to hold the door ajar. Slammed it hard into the dwarf's mouth, as teeth caught at it and sinews, possibly the mandible, gave. Lodged it there.

I had a dim, peripheral perception of others standing just inside the door, watching.

I got up onto my knees. Blood ran down my face. I tossed my head to clear it out of my eyes. My lower back throbbed with pain and for days, whenever I peed, the water in the bowl went red.

"Where's Alouette?"

"Man, if we knew, we'd tell you."

This was from the tall guy, kind of grunting it out, hugging his nuts with both hands.

"Go on."

"She be here a coupla times. Been a while."

"How long?"

No response. I set the heel of my hand against the wedge and drove it in deeper. This time the mandible gave for sure.

"Jesus, man," Silky said. "I don't know. A week, maybe two."

"Mrff, gdfftm, lfft," the dwarf said. Blood bubbled up out of his nose when he breathed.

"You didn't have to do that," Silky said.

Probably not.

I stopped off at the Clarksville Regional ER for stitches and X rays. Nothing was broken, but everything hurt like hell. What else was new? I declined Tylenol 3, went back to my room, swallowed half a handful of aspirin and poured three fingers of scotch into the plastic cup. Watched part of a movie about child abuse. Poured another drink. Fell asleep there in the chair.

Then someone was pounding at my door.

I opened it. Sergeant Travis had two quart-size Styrofoam containers of coffee balanced piggyback in one hand, a paper bag of doughnuts in the other.

"Thought you might could use this."

He held out the cups so I could take one and came on in. Put the bag on the dresser. The TV was still on and he sat watching a Tom and Jerry cartoon and sipping at coffee. I did the same.

"Your name kind of came up, Griffin."

"Names have a way of doing that."

"Made me wonder enough that I called your friend on the force in New Orleans, Walsh, and talked to him about you. He told me if he sent you out to the corner for a paper, chances would be about fifty-fifty of his actually getting one, but that he'd trust you with his life. One of your stranger character references."

"Two of your stranger characters."

He finished his coffee and dropped the cup into the trashcan. "You guys go back a ways, huh?"

"There's history, yes."

"You want one of these?" He'd snagged the bag of doughnuts and pulled one out. Chewed on it a moment and dropped it into the trashcan too. "Damn things always *look* so good. But they taste like sugared cardboard and turn into fists in your gut somewhere. Thing is, we had a report of probable assault from the hospital—"

"I made no such complaint."

"Didn't have to. We like to stay on top of things around here, Griffin. Man comes into ER all beat to hell, the staff's just naturally going to let me know about it."

"They're not big fans of legal fine points such as patient confidentiality, I take it."

"Well you know, city people are the ones that seem always to be worried about protecting their anonymity.

Maybe that has something to do with *why* they're city people. Town this size, everybody tends to know everybody else's business anyway. This has to be one of the new ones,'' he said, nodding toward the TV. ''The old ones were rough as a cob—jerky and poorly drawn, violent—but they had a magic to them somehow.''

He shook his head sadly for all lost things.

''So I hear about this apparent assault and I have to wonder if there might be a connection between that and an incident out on county road one-seventeen a little earlier. Because someone big and black swooped in there like some kind of avenging angel—avenging what, no one knows—and beat the bejesus out of a couple of our self-employed businessmen. One of them's having his jaw wired about now, gonna be getting tired of liquids pretty soon. People who were watching said this guy just walked up and took them down, just like that, no reason or anything.''

''There was probably reason.''

''Yeah.'' His eyes hadn't left the TV, where a cat, chasing a mouse, crossed offscreen right to offscreen left and moments later came fleeing back across, pursued by the mouse. ''Probably so. Look: Walsh tells me you're okay, I'm willing to go along with that, at least until I see different. But if you're going to be running around busting jaws, I need to know now.''

''Things got a little out of hand.''

''Things have a way of doing just that. What I want is for you to tell me you're going to be able to keep that hand closed, so things don't get out of it anymore.''

I nodded.

''I'll bust you quick as I will anyone else, if it comes to that, friends or no friends. And whether I personally want to or not. The point could come. You understand that, don't you?''

''Yes.''

''So I'm trusting you to walk carefully, and watch your back. Especially watch your back. Camaro didn't have any way of knowing you were going to go in there and John Wayne those boys all to shit, or he wouldn't have sent you out there. But those boys have a lot of business associates.''

''Also self-employed.''

''Yeah, well, it does tend to be an at-home kind of industry. But I'm saying they might take it personally, some of the others. Especially if they find you getting in their faces again.''

''I understand.''

''Take care then, Griffin. You get in too deep, you give me a call.''

''So you can lead a cavalry charge?''

He laughed. ''Hell no. So I can step back out of the way.''

20

WHENEVER THINGS BEGIN TO LOOK ABSOLUTELY, UN-remittingly impossible and I find myself sinking into despair for myself and the human race, I read Thomas Bernhard. It always cheers me up. No one is more bitter, no one has ever lived in a bleaker world than Thomas Bernhard.

The only contender is Jonathan Swift, whose epitaph might do as well for Bernhard: "He has gone where fierce indignation can lacerate his heart no more."

All Bernhard's work is visible struggle: invectives against his Austrian homeland, combats occurring solely within the human mind and imagination, blustery dialogues that finally surrender pretense and paragraphs to become clotted, hundred-page soliloquies. And beneath it all, his certainty that language above all embodies humanity's refusal to accept the world as it is, that it is a machinery of essential falsehoods and fabrications.

Unable to get back to sleep following Sergeant Travis's visit that afternoon, having no Thomas Bernhard at hand and little prospect of finding any there in the hinterestlands, I did the next-best thing. I made a cemetery run.

Confederate cemeteries are scattered throughout the South, some with only a half-dozen or dozen gravesites, others sprawling over the equivalent of a city block. They're often grand places, with elaborate headstones and inscriptions, generally well-kept and -visited. And one of the most celebrated, I knew, was not far from Clarksville.

It was almost dark when I got there. You turned off the highway just past Faith Baptist Church (I stopped twice along the way to ask), drove down a narrow asphalt road (pulling to the shoulder whenever vehicles appeared on the other side) and onto a wider dirt one, then through a modern graveyard of low headstones and bright green grass into a copse where half-lifesize statues of soldiers reared up among the trees. Still farther along lay a separate Negro graveyard with wooden markers.

The trees were mostly magnolias, mostly dormant now. Clusters of leaves, still green but curiously unalive, hung as though holding their breath, waiting.

Marble and cement soldiers, horses, angels, beloved dogs, pylons, pinnacles, sad women.

A squat obelisk of veined marble bearing the figure of a child, though he wore an officer's uniform: *Let Us Remember That After Midnight Cometh Morn.*

A casket-shaped headstone with a central spire of wrought iron: *Honor. Family. Faith.*

And on a small, simple marker hand-carved to resemble a scroll, far more appropriate to New Orleans (where it would have indicated the young man died in a duel, not war): *Mort sur le champ d'honneur.*

Poor ol' Tom Jefferson with his slave mistress Sally Hemings and his two hundred slaves at Monticello and his denouncements of slavery as a great political and moral evil, knowing all the time he would suffer economic ruin if his own slaves were freed. And that the neighbors would talk something awful.

Life, Mr. Jefferson, is an unqualified, neo-Marxist bitch.

Everything comes down to simple economics, however fine-spirited we are.

Looking up, I saw that a white boy of twelve or so stood off at the side of the field with a shotgun cradled in his arms, watching me.

I nodded his way.

He nodded back and kept watching.

As Robert Johnson said: Sun goin' down, boy, dark gon' catch me here.

Maybe not a good idea, even this late in the American game. So I mounted my Mazda and rode into the sunset, leaving the dead, those dead, forever behind.

21

BABY GIRL MCTELL DIED ON NOVEMBER 19TH, ON A
starless, overcast morning, a little after 2:00 A.M.

The phone in my motel room dredged me from sleep.
Topmost levels of my mind came instantly awake; I
waited as others drifted up to join them. Lights from a
car in the lot outside made a shadow screen of my wall,
everything outsize and tipped at odd angles as in old
German Expressionist films. The car's idle was set too
low; every few seconds it began sputtering out and the
driver had to tap the gas pedal.

"Yeah?" I said.

"Mr. Griffin?"

I said yes, and Doctor Arellano told me they had done
all they could.

I thanked him, said I'd be in later to see to arrange-
ments, and hung up. There was nothing to drink, or I
would have drunk it. Outside, a car door slammed and
a woman shouted, as the car pulled away, Damn you!
You hear me? God damn you!

I splashed water on my face and sat for a while staring
out into the darkness with late-night radio blathering behind me. Then I turned on water in the shower to give
it time to warm while I shaved. I was climbing in when
the phone rang again.

"Lew? Teresa. Becky Walden just called. The nurse
who was taking care of our girl tonight. She knew I'd
want to know. I'm so sorry, Lew."

I watched dampness spread slowly over the carpet at
my feet.

"Lew, are you okay?"

"Fine." Clearing my throat, I said it again.

"Listen, it's my night off. Would you like me to come over? Maybe it's not a good idea for you to be alone tonight. I'm up anyway—I can't ever sleep like a normal person, even on my nights off—and watching old movies. I could be right there, provided you don't mind stay-at-home old clothes and aboriginal hair. There's no sense in your going in to the hospital till morning, anyway. None of the administrators are there before nine."

"I'd like you here," I said after a moment.

"Then I'm on my way."

Her stay-at-home old clothes turned out to be designer, French and recently pressed. The aboriginal hair looked pretty much the way it always did.

Myself, I'd barely managed a dash through the shower, jeans and a T-shirt.

"Lew," she said when I opened the door, "I'd like you to meet Beth Ann, the only reason I'm still here in the States. I hope you don't mind my bringing her along."

Her companion was a stunning, tall woman with light brown skin, golden eyes and elaborate Old South manners. She took my hand and seemed for a moment on the verge of curtsying.

"Beth Ann's from Charleston. She's never been able to quite get over it."

"Now that I've seen her, I'd be surprised if Charleston ever got over *her*."

"What did I tell you?" Teresa said to Beth Ann.

"You told me he was a good-looking charmer. And you were at least half right."

"Does the word coquettish come to mind?" Teresa asked me.

"Among others," I said. Mutual admiration was flowing thick in there. Pretty soon we'd have to hack our way through it with machetes.

"I'm sorry about the little girl, Mr. Griffin."

"Lew. And thank you. Though I guess it's what we all had to expect."

"That doesn't make it any easier."

"No. No, it doesn't."

Teresa lowered a paper bag onto the dresser and reached in, pulling out three mugs, each fitted with its own lid. She handed one to each of us, kept one herself. Mine was so hot I could hardly hold on to it.

"Mistake," Teresa said. "Trade. This is coffee: yours. B.A. and I have tea."

"Tea's wonderful. Split it with me?"

"Of course. But I didn't know you were a tea drinker. You've always had coffee."

"When in Rome," I said.

"Quite."

I had never told her about Vicky. Now I did.

"You loved her," Teresa said when I finished.

"Oh yes."

"And you let her go."

"The way one lets the wind blow, or the sun come up. She made her own choices, her own decisions. There wasn't much I could do."

"There are always things we can do, Lew. You could have gone back with her. She asked."

I shook my head, much as I had done all those years ago. I handed Teresa the mug. She drank and passed it back.

"Do you hear from her?"

"I did, for a while. Less and less as time went on. She had a family, a son, a busy husband doing important things, a new daughter. And her own career, of course. Ties loosen. Memories get hung on walls or put away in the corners of drawers and life goes on."

Teresa held out the almost-empty mug and, when I shook my head, drank off the last swig of tea herself. Then she pried the lid off the coffee, sipped, passed it on to me. We were all sitting on a long plastic-covered couch under the picture window with its theater-curtain

drape, looking at cinderblock painted green and light
from the bathroom spilling out over brown carpeting.

"You miss her," Teresa said.

"I miss a lot of things—"

"She wasn't a thing, Lew."

"—but the train keeps moving on."

"When I was ten," Beth Ann said, "my sister, the
one who raised me after my folks died, put me on a train
to Chicago, to see my grandparents. I'd never been out
of Charleston, never been much of anywhere but home
and the Catholic school I attended. I was scared to death.
I didn't even know there were bathrooms on the train.
And I was starved. I'd left home at six in the morning
without breakfast and everybody around me now was
eating chicken or sandwiches out of bags and boxes. I
hadn't moved this whole time. I was just sitting there,
half a step from peeing my pants, when a conductor
walked up. I'll never forget him. A white man, in his
thirties I guess, though he seemed horribly old at the
time. And he just said: Come with me, girl. Took me
back to the club car, showed me where the bathroom
was, the one he and the other employees used. And the
rest of that trip he kept bringing me ham sandwiches.
Just a slice of ham, two pieces of white bread and may-
onnaise, but they tasted better than anything else I'd ever
had in my life."

We'd long ago finished the coffee, but had kept passing the mug back and forth in one of those spontaneous,
unspoken inspirations that occasionally arise. Whoever
held the mug (we now realized, all at once) had to speak.

Teresa: "Many women have loved you, Lew."

Beth Ann: "Life could be worthwhile without Terri,
I know that. There would be reasons to go on living. I
would find them. But right now I can't imagine what
they might be."

Teresa: "Coming here, to the States to live—for a
single year, I thought then—I felt as Columbus must
have felt. I was falling off the edge of the world, leaving

civilization behind me. Then I discovered malls! fast food! credit cards!''

Me: "Once in the sixties I remember seeing spray-painted on the wall of a K&B: Convenience Kills.''

Teresa: " 'For arrogance and hatred are the wares peddled in the thoroughfares.' ''

B.A.: "Yeats.''

Me: " 'A Poem for My Daughter.' Now *I'm* the fifty-year-old, unsmiling, unpublic man.''

"I think we need to give some thought to food,'' Teresa said. "Food seems essential.''

"I think we're all still waiting for that conductor,'' Beth Ann said.

22

The sun was edging up by the time we climbed into Teresa's car to head for a restaurant out on the loop. I sat between her and Beth Ann in the front seat. Morning light filled our conversation, too; shadows fell away. When they dropped me back at the motel an hour or so later, after two pecan waffles and a gallon of coffee, I'd begun filling slowly with light myself.

I showered, put on real clothes (Verne called them "grown-up clothes," I suddenly remembered) and went to the hospital to see what I needed to do. Day Administrator Katherine Farrell, a woman in her late fifties and more handsome than pretty, striking nonetheless, expressed her condolences and said that Mrs. Adams had already signed the necessary papers.

I found her sitting in the covered bus stop outside the hospital. I sat down beside her. We watched traffic go by.

"Ain't the first or the last time either of us lost something," she said after a while.

"No, m'am."

A workhorse of an old Ford pickup, fenders ripped away, heaved past, wearing the latest of several coats of primer. A beetle-green new Toyota followed close behind. Rap's heavy iambs, its booming bass, washed over us.

"I want you to know I've been talking to those nurses in there. They tell me you loved that little girl, that you're a good man. And judging from what you said on the way here, my daughter turned out a fair good woman."

"Yes, m'am. She did. She always was."

"Been wrong before."

"Yes, m'am." Then, after a moment, nothing more forthcoming: "Thank you."

I stood. "My car's in the lot, Mrs. Adams. I'll drive you back home now, if you're ready."

She put her hand out and I took it. It was like holding on to dry twigs.

"I'd appreciate that, Lewis," she said.

I was back in Clarksville by midafternoon and, after a quick meal at a place called The Drop, stretched out at the motel for a few hours' sleep. I'd got almost half of one of those hours when the phone rang.

I struggled to the surface and said, "Yeah?"

"Sorry about the kid. I know how that feels, and that nothing I can say's going to help. You know who this is, right?"

I nodded, then came a little more awake and said, "Camaro." The world was swimming into focus, albeit soft.

"You okay, man?"

"Fine. Just haven't managed much sleep this last couple of days."

"Know how that is, too. I can call back."

"No reason to. What's up?"

"Well . . ." It rolled on out for half a minute or so. "Probably shouldn't be calling you at all. Last time I did, from what I hear, you went apeshit and ralphed those boys right into the hospital. You ever hear of asking a guy first?"

"I asked."

"Oh yeah? Remember to say please?"

"I'm sure I did. Rarely forget that. I may have left off the thank you, though, now that I think about it."

"Ever had your jaw wired, Griffin?"

"Came close a few times."

"I bet you did. Probably chew the wires up and spit them at people. Well, what the fuck, those boys are pretty much garbage anyway. You don't take them out to the curb, someone else will."

"So: you called up to give me a few hot tips on navigating the complex social waters of postcolonial Mississippi. Or just to chat, for old times' sake? Not that we share any old times."

"We all know you're *bad* by now, Griffin."

"Yeah, well, I need sleep more than I need bullshit right now."

"You also need help finding your girl. Though damn if *I* know why anyone'd want to help you."

"It's my honest face. My purity of heart. My high position in antebellum society. And the twenties I spread around. What do you have?"

"Thought you always remembered to say please."

"Please."

"There's a girl, Louette, that's been kind of living at this dealer's house just over the state line. I mean, they finally took a look around and realized she's been there at least a month. Helping out at first you know, doing the guys when they were able or whatever, but since then just hunkering down there, riding a big free one. Even *they* know that's not good business."

"Thank you."

I wrote down the address he gave me.

"One thing," he said.

"Yeah?"

"Try to keep from going nuclear on this one? You're not in the big city now. We try to keep a lower profile out here, now draw too much attention to ourselves."

I told him I'd do what I could. Neither of us believed it.

The house was up in West Memphis, on the outskirts, in a part of town owing its existence to the spillover from Memphis military bases during World War II, a warren of apartment-size simple wood homes set close in row after row like carrots in a garden. Narrow, bobtail driveways had eroded through the years, cowlicks of grass and hedge pushing through them; many of the carports had become extra rooms, utility sheds, screened-in porches; trailers were grafted onto some. Abandoned refrigerators, motorcycles and decaying cars sat in yards beside swing sets and inflatable pools.

I pulled to the curb at 3216 Zachary Taylor. Out my side window in the distance I could see the wing-like curve of the Arkansas-Mississippi Bridge. I'd had to drive on into Memphis, drop onto Riverfront Drive, and loop back across the bridge into Arkansas. I started up the brief walk, hearing what sounded like reggae country music from inside. Marley in Nashville, maybe. Jimmy Cliff and His Country Shitkickers.

Remembering Camaro's admonitions, I knocked politely at the door. No one responded, so I knocked, politely, again. Then, with still no response, as politely as possible I started kicking.

The door opened and a man maybe half my age stood there. Brush-style blond hair, fatigue pants with a white Hanes T, lizard cowboy boots. Pumper muscles and an earring. Tumbler in hand. Tequila, from the smell of it.

"What is your *prob*lem?"

Behind him, from different rooms, both Randy Travis and reggae were playing at high volume, crashing onto one another's beach, from time to time blending in an oddly beautiful way.

"Oh. Sorry. Didn't think you'd heard me."

"We heard you. They heard you over in Little Rock, man."

"Good. It's so hard to be heard in this world. Thank you."

"Mama brought you up right, did she? Manners like that, I'd think you couldn't be anything but one of those biblebeaters that come through here every week or so. They're always wearing a coat and tie, too. Don't nobody *else* 'round here."

He took a sip of his drink.

"But of course you ain't no biblebeater, are you?"

"No sir, I have to tell you I'm not. But I do wonder if you might do me the favor of answering a question or two. I won't trouble you to take much of your time."

"And why would I answer any questions you'd have? Unless you have a warrant, that is."

"Warrant?"

"Come on, you got cop on you like slime on a snail."

Another, shorter man with a close-cut helmet of hair, vaguely elfish, had joined him at the door. Squinting beneath monumental eyebrows he said, "Yeah, man, this the *new* South. Nigger cops ever'-where."

"You go on back inside now, Bobo. We're doing just fine out here."

"So that's the way it is here in America. What made us great," he said to me. "You come back with a warrant, or the next time it's clear trespass. You hear what I'm saying?"

Uh-oh. This guy watched cop shows; I was in trouble.

He shut the door.

When it stopped against my foot, he glanced down.

Then he looked back up at me and, for a split second before he caught himself, over my shoulder.

It was enough.

I went down, rolling, as the guy behind me swung and, meeting no resistance, connected with Mr. Warrant midchest, a glancing blow, then toppled himself.

I pivoted back like a break dancer and slammed

my feet into Warrant's kidneys. His glass bounced off the front wall and rebounded, spinning, into the small entryway, came up against vinyl coping and stopped there, rocking back and forth. I hooked fingers into his neck now that he was down. Put a heel hard against the other one's balls and felt him curl in on himself.

"Your call," I told him. "Funny how so much of life comes down to attitude, huh?"

"Hold on, man," he said. "We can talk about this." And the minute I started backing off his windpipe and carotid: *"Bobby Ray!"*

Who trotted in from a room to the right where the face of some talk-show host filled a TV screen like an egg in a bottle, nailing live audience and viewers with sincere clear eyes.

Bobby Ray had a sincere Walther PPK in one hand.

I had a coat rack.

It caught him full across neck and chest. Remember Martin Balsam pedaling backward down the stairs in *Psycho*?

His head came up off the floor like a turtle's, trying for air. Didn't get it. The head went back down. He was still.

I set the coat rack back down in the corner. A few well-anchored coats swung to a stop on its hooks; most were on the floor.

"You have a right not to move," I told Mr. Warrant. "You get up and I use you to clean furniture. You hear what I'm saying?"

He nodded.

I picked up the PPK and walked into the next room. Faces turned toward me. Petals on a wet black bough. A modest buffet of drugs was set out on a card table: joints, bowls of colored pills, a couple of small covered plastic containers, a marble cheese board with razor and some remains of white powder on it.

Feeding time at the zoo.

"Our savior."

"Ecce homo. And I do mean mo'."

"Show-and-tell time, obviously."

"Black's definitely beautiful."

"Validate your parking ticket, sir?"

"Pizza dude's here."

"Help."

Alouette said nothing.

I found her in the back bedroom, lying on two stacked mattresses, nude, between a skinny black man and a fat 44-D blonde. They were passing a fifth of Southern Comfort back and forth over her. The *Green Acres* theme erupted from a bedside TV.

I dug into the hollow of her neck. There was a pulse, albeit a weak one.

"Where's the phone?"

He looked at me and, without looking away, handed the bottle across to the blonde. She grappled and found it, hauled it in, breast swinging.

In one continuous move I took it from her and smashed it against the headboard. Held a most satisfying handle and bladelike shard of glass against the man's throat as I watched his hard-on dwindle to nothing, with the impossibly sweet reek of oranges washing over us.

"Now," I said.

His eyes swept toward the floor. Again, again. I reached under the bed and pulled out the phone. Dialed 911.

"Thirty-two sixteen Zachary Taylor," I said. Overdose, I was going to say, but heard instead: "Officer down." There'd be hell to pay. But the ambulance was there in four minutes.

While we were waiting, new muscle came into the room. Three of them.

"That's the guy did Lonnie," one of them said. "Busted his jaw."

"Son of a bitch."

"Oyster time."

I lifted the PPK.

We were still facing one another off when the ambulance and four police cars careened into place.

23

TIME TO REMEMBER LOTS OF PRISON FILMS. LISPING Tony Curtis chained to a black stud, spoon handles ground down to knives against cement floors, lights dimming all over town as Big Lou got fried moments before the stay of execution came, college students on summer vacation in the South pulled over by big-bellied cops and railroaded onto chain gangs. And the novels: Malcolm Braly's *On the Yard*, Chester Himes's *Cast the First Stone*.

On the way in, in the squad car, one of the cops asked me what the hell I thought I was doing.

A good question.

A *very* good question for this fifty-year-old, unsmiling, resolutely unpublic man.

What *was* I doing?

Besides sitting in a holding cell in West Memphis, Arkansas, that is—home at last, or close enough.

Besides not telling mostly indifferent juniors, seniors and a scatter of grad students about modern French novels—which is what I was *supposed* to be doing.

The thought occurred to me that I'd disappeared from my school as precipitately and incommunicably as, a few years ago, my son David had vanished from his.

I really *was* getting far too old for this.

And besides, basically the whole thing just wasn't any of my business.

And so I sat there, watching dawn lightly brush, then nudge, then fill a single high window, drinking cup after cup of coffee deputies brought me and declining their offer of cigarettes, my mind curving gently inward, backward, toward things long shut away.

David: his final postcard and consummate disappearance, those moments of silence on the phone machine's tape.

Vicky: red hair drifting in a cloud above me, pale white body opening beneath me, trilled r's, unvoiced assents, *I can't do this any longer Lew*. Seeing her off and for the last time at the airport as she emplaned for Paris.

LaVerne.

Till the drifting mind fetched up, finally, on a shore of sorts.

I thought of two photos of my parents, the only things I'd kept when Francy and I went through the house after Mom died. After these, taken the year they were married, they became shy; only a handful of snapshots remain, and in them, in every case, my parents are turned, or turning, away from the camera: looking off, averting faces, moving toward the borders of the frame. But here my mother, then in a kind of mirror image my father, sit on the hood of a Hudson Terraplane, so that, were the photos placed side by side, they would be looking into one another's eyes. And that image—their occupancy of discrete worlds, the connection relying upon careful placement, upon circumstance—seems wholly appropriate in light of their subsequent life together, Chekhov's precisely wrong and telling detail.

All their silent, ceaseless warfare came later, of course. Here in these photos, momentarily, the world has softened. She is full of life, a plainly pretty woman for whom life is just now beginning. His mixed heritage shows in cheekbones and straight, jet-black hair; his skin is light, like Charlie Patton's. They are a handsome, a fine, young couple.

As I myself grew older, into my early teens, I began to notice that my father was slowly going out of focus, blurring at the edges, color washing out to the dun

grayish-green of early Polaroids. I can't be sure this is
how I saw it at the time; time's whispers are suspect,
memory forever as much poet as reporter; and perhaps
this is only the way that, retrospectively, imaginatively,
I make sense for now (though a limited sense, true) of
what then bewildered me.

My mother by then had already begun her own de-
cline, her own transformation, hardening into a bitter
rind of a woman who pushed through the stations of her
day as though each moment were unpleasant duty; as
though the currencies of joy had become so inflated they
could no longer purchase anything of worth.

How had those two young people on the Terraplane
ever become the sad, embattled, barricaded couple I
grew up with? What terrible, quiet things had happened
to them?

How do *any* of us become what we are, really: so
distant a thing from what we set out to be, and seemed?

How, for instance, does a part-time college instructor,
part-time novelist who believed he'd put his past behind
him where it rightfully belonged (and what he couldn't
put behind him, into his books), come to be sitting in
an interrogation room across from a quartet of cops at
nine in the morning in West Memphis, Arkansas?

Which is where I was but minutes later.

The guy who seemed to be in charge had oiled-down
hair, a bushy mustache and rolled-up sleeves. I felt a
moment's terror that a barbershop quartet had been sent
in to interrogate me. Any moment they were going to
start singing "The Whiffenpoof Song," and I'd tell
them everything I knew. Hell, I'd tell them things I
didn't know. As a writer, I was good at that.

"Can we get you anything, Mr. Griffin, before we
start?"

Had to be the baritone. He and a wiry little guy, probably the tenor, sat at the table. The others sat against the
wall behind them on folding chairs. The table between
us had nothing on it. Table, floor and walls were spot-

less, scrubbed. The air smelled faintly of disinfectant and lemon.

"No, but thanks."

"Then could you explain to us why on the emergency line you represented yourself as a police officer?"

I tried to think of a snappy response. Marlowe certainly would have had one.

"Strictly speaking, I didn't," was the best I could do.

" 'Officer down,' I believe you said."

That kind of set the pace for the whole thing. They'd ask a question and I'd answer it, they'd ask another and circle back to an earlier one. It was a lot like the chants kids use when they're jumping rope. Or gamelan music.

"I needed help fast. The girl was in bad shape."

We were all very polite, very businesslike. There were things, practical things, to get done, and we were men of the world. Members of the quartet changed from time to time. Toward the end, two hours or more into the morning, Sergeant Travis of Clarksville's finest came in and sat against the back wall.

"You went there for a drug buy and the deal went bad," one of them was saying just then. "We know that, Griffin."

I looked across at Travis. He shook his head sadly, looked at the floor.

This went on a while, as it had been going on, and eventually Travis stood, nodded to me, and left. I had become a tape loop.

Ten minutes later he walked back in behind a guy in a suit and said, "Come on, Griffin, let's go."

I followed him out into a long bare hallway, voices raised and clashing behind us.

"Last I heard, extradition didn't work like this."

"All in who and what you know," Travis said. "Those boys are kind of pissed, right now. They've been planning a raid on that house for three weeks. It was finally set to go down tonight. And here you went and spoiled their party. Luckily, Douglas and I went to

high school together. Guy in the suit? He's the chief
here. Caught a hundred long passes from that man if I
caught one. You play?''

"Hate football." Didn't dance, either.

"Look like you could have, easy."

We were standing outside the station now. I felt
strangely weightless. Travis stopped and turned toward
me.

"They're not charging you with anything. But god-
al*mighty* are they pissed."

"Give me a lift?"

"Be glad to, but you don't need one."

He smiled. Handed me an envelope: wallet, pocket
contents, keys.

"Your car's in the lot around back. I had a trustee go
out there and bring it in."

"I don't suppose you want to tell me how it was that
you happened to show up here?"

"Not really. But in my experience, there's very little
in life that just happens. Know what I mean?"

"No. And I don't guess I'm going to."

"Doesn't matter. You'll be coming back down to
Clarksville?"

"I don't know. Not right away, at any rate. There may
be no reason to. First I have to find out about Alouette."

We'd walked around to the back. I opened the car
door and reached to shake his hand.

"Thanks. I appreciate what you've done." Whatever
the reasons.

"The girl's over at Baptist Hospital, tenth floor.
Across the bridge, find Union Avenue and you're almost
there. She's going to be okay, Griffin. For now, anyway."

I got in and started the engine.

"Thanks again, Sergeant."

"Nothing to it."

"Tell Camaro thanks for me, too, when you see
him?"

"I'll do that. If I see him, you understand."

It's still a hell of a river, even if it did seem bigger when I was a kid: not only endless, but also impossibly wide. It was full of boats then, with sandbars the size of islands; and ferries nosed back and forth across the wake of the big ships, cars crouched on their decks, people peering out from within, waiting for things to change.

24

HOSPITALS, LIKE BUS STATIONS AND PRISONS, ARE ALL much the same. Their makers conjure up the soul of the thing, then drape skin around it. This one was like the one where I woke all those years ago, light like fists in my eyes, with Vicky's face hovering over me; like the one unseen in which my father died; like the one that broke Cordelia Davis's long fall; like the one in which Verne had lain dying.

Tenth floor was a limited-admittance wing, and after being turned away at the nurse's station I had to go back down to the administrative offices, where the atmosphere was so different that it was like stepping into another world, to clear permissions. I gave my name and relationship to Alouette to a walleyed young man whose expression suggested that he found what he saw out here perpetually just beyond his understanding, and added that he might call Travis for corroboration.

"Oh that won't be necessary, Mr. Griffin," he said, handing a small paper across to me. "Sergeant Travis has already called. Let me wish you and the girl both the best of luck. It's tough, I know."

I shared the ride back up with a stretcher and two attendants, probably a nurse and respiratory therapist. An old lady with skin like dried mud flats lay on the stretcher surrounded by monitors, oxygen cylinder, IV bags and portable pump, a compact drug box, charts, a box of disposable diapers. Tubes and drains snaked out from under the sheet covering her. She was trached, and the attendant at the head of the stretcher was squeezing an Ambu bag regularly, monotonously, to give her breath. Her eyes locked on to mine and I was surprised at how clear, how filled with intelligence, they were. Those eyes followed me as I got off on the tenth floor.

I handed over my scrip to the nurse at the gateway. She'd summon Charon, who'd ferry me across. But she only looked at it and signaled to another beyond the double doors. That one buzzed the doors to unlock them, holding her finger on the button until I was in.

A young woman sitting behind the desk just inside stood. "Mr. Griffin?" She was in her midtwenties, a blonde with perfect fair skin and a bow in her hair. Typical valley girl sort, but she was wearing jeans, cowboy boots and a denim shirt with snaps for buttons. Barbie at the Bar-B, I thought inanely.

She held out a hand to shake mine. "I'm Mickey Francis, a social worker on the staff here. We don't have very much information about Alouette, I'm afraid. Do you have a few minutes to answer some questions? It would be a great help to us."

"I have the time, Miss Francis. But I don't know if I'll have any answers for you."

"Anything will help."

So we went down the hall to a conference room looking much like the police interrogation room back across the river, poured two cups of coffee and sat down. A calendar on the wall showed a swatch of New England forest in the throes of fall, an impossible array of gold and scarlet and chrome yellow; each leaf on each tree seemed a different color. Starting with Chip Landrieu's arrival at my doorstep, backtracking to Verne's and my lengthy relationship, jump-cutting forward to Baby Girl's death, I told her what I knew.

As I talked, she made brief notes in a pocket memo book. I thought of Eddie Lang, who kept the cues for the entire Whiteman Orchestra repertoire on an index card. And of how he had tried so hard, in those amazing duets with Lonnie Johnson, to transcend his heavy, European style. Lang could hear the difference, that loose urgency, in Johnson's playing—sensed but somehow couldn't seize it.

"Do you mind if I contact Richard Garces?" she asked when I finished. "He might be able to get some of the information we need. Legally I suppose we're going to have to notify the father, but we can probably hold off on that for a while."

"When you do, be prepared for the descent of the Valkyries."

"Oh, we're used to Valkyries around here, Mr. Griffin." She stood and held out her hand. "Thank you for your help. We'll do what we can. But as you know, Alouette will have to do most of it herself. Jane, at the desk, will take you in to see her. The police have cleared her from the jail ward, by the way: she'll be moved to a regular ICU as soon as a bed comes available. Good luck."

She walked away. Because the boots' heels tipped her forward and she leaned back just a little too hard against it, she seemed above the waist to carry herself stiffly and unnaturally straight. But her legs, long and looking still longer in jeans and heels, moved freely.

Jane escorted me into a four-bed room just within the double doors. To the right, propped on his or her side with rolled pillows, lay a hairless individual with intersecting scars like two zippers across the crown of his/her head. He or she was trached, and an aerosol generator in the wall above the bed, hissing, delivered continuous humidity to the airway through a corrugated tube and T-piece, outflow disappearing when the patient breathed in, spuming back into the room on exhalation. In the bed behind this one, a middle-aged woman sat upright, eyes following my progress into the room, face and eyes equally blank.

Alouette was in the rear left corner, past an unoccupied bed. Soft restraints at ankles and wrists were tied to the bed rails, and a half dozen sandbags chucked along her sides helped hold her in place, so that she could move only her eyes. Towels covered breasts and abdomen. She had peripheral IVs in each arm, happy-face patches for the cardiac monitor on her chest, yet another line in her neck. An endotracheal tube was taped in place at her mouth and connected to a ventilator alongside the bed. Its bellows rose, hesitated and fell, accordionlike.

A nurse had just finished bathing her and was gathering up the plastic basin half filled with water, washcloths, talcum, bottle of liquid soap, toothbrush, toothpaste. "Are you the father?"

I shook my head. "A friend."

Alouette's eyes had locked on to me. I imagined that I saw all sorts of things in them. Perhaps I did. She tried to speak, prompting a loud buzz and flashing light from the ventilator.

"You can't talk, sweetheart, remember?"

She put down the basin and reached for a clipboard on the bedside table.

"I'll undo an arm, honey, if you promise me you won't try to pull anything loose. And then I can leave you folks alone a minute."

Alouette looked at her and blinked several times.

"You'll have to help her," the nurse said to me. "Things are still pretty thin for her. Will be, for a while."

She started to untie her right arm, but when I told her that Alouette was left-handed (like her mother), she re-did the knot and pulled the other free instead. Handed me the clipboard.

I walked around to the side and held it up for her, gave her the pencil. She made several tries at it—lines huge and shaky and often not meeting, other times over-scoring one another, tip of the pencil lead breaking away at one point—before I could make out what it was.

LEW.

I nodded, surprised that she knew who I was.

I—
Hope? Hate?
She tried again.
No: Hurt.
I HURT.
And what I said then, unintended, unexpectedly, came
in a rush.

25

I HAD BEEN IN NEW ORLEANS A LITTLE MORE THAN A year when I met your mother. I was a fatback-and-grits kid from Arkansas who'd read a few books and thought they'd taught him whatever secrets he needed to know. I had this black gabardine suit that I'd wear all the time, press it and one of my three shirts every morning, put on a tie of some kind, buff my shoes with a towel. I wasn't drinking much, then. That came later. But I always tried to look presentable.

I'd been in and out of several jobs by that time. Bell-hopped at the Royal Orleans for a little while, worked the ticket counter at the bus station, even did some short-order cooking and janitored at a grade school when times got really hard. I was living with half a dozen or more people, the number kept changing from week to week, or even day to day, in a house on Dryades, an old camelback double. People used to kid me because everywhere I went I wore that suit.

I was sitting at the counter in a diner one morning about four, nursing a cup of coffee, wearing my suit. I'd been fired the day before for "talking back" to my supervisor (actually, I'd told him to go to hell), and I left the store, went out and got drunk by midafternoon, somehow got home and passed out there till thirst and jittery nerves shook me awake a little before midnight.

Someone sat down beside me. When I looked at her, she smiled, sipped her coffee and said "Nice suit."

I thanked her, and after a moment she said, "Things kind of slow for you tonight too, I guess."

And that was your mother, the first time I ever saw her. And that's all we said. But the next night I was there at that same diner from two to six, and the *next* night she came in, around five, and sat down by me again when she saw me, and we talked. So then we started having breakfast together most mornings. And after a couple of weeks I asked her to have dinner with me that night. "You mean like a date?" she said. And I said, "Yeah, like a date."

By the end of the month I'd had two more jobs, quit one and got fired from the other, and had moved in with her on a more or less permanent basis. She helped me get another job, someone she knew from her work knew someone else, that kind of thing. It was with this furniture and appliance outfit over on Magazine. They'd sell all this stuff on time at inflated prices and have people sign contracts agreeing to forfeit everything if there was ever a missed payment. Mostly poor black people, and most of them not even able to read the contracts. But the company was considerate. They always sent their man around to try to collect before they were forced "to invoke the terms of contract." And I was their man.

So I'd go humping all over town doing what I could to help these people keep their things. I'd explain what the contract said, tell them if they didn't scrape a payment together by Friday, or Monday, or whatever, the truck would back up to their door and haul it all away and they'd *still* owe the company money for whatever payments were outstanding at the time of repossession. A couple of times I even threw in some of my own money.

Then one day the owner wants to see me in his office. "You doin' okay, Lew?" he says. Then he tells me word's got to him how I've been going about my collections, that I know damn well that's not the way it's done and he never wanted to hire me in the first place, and I had better get my black butt in the groove or out of his store, did I understand.

It went on like that a little while, not too much longer. Finally I just reached across the desk, pulled him toward me by his shirtfront and started pounding at his face. Afterwards, I went on home.

The police picked me up within the hour. I was sitting out on the porch, cleaned up and dressed in my black suit and waiting for them. The officers and I were polite. A few days later, the judge was polite. He said, politely, that I had a choice: prison for assault and battery, or the armed services, who might be able to put to some good use my, ah, talent for mayhem. A squad car delivered me directly from courtroom to recruiter who, once I'd signed papers, took over. I never even had chance to call your mother.

It didn't last long. The army didn't think I was nearly as desirable as that judge had. And when I got out, your mother was there at the bus station in New Orleans waiting for me. Wearing, since she was working that night, a blue satin dress and blood-red heels, and looking unbelievably beautiful.

After that, we were together, even when we were apart, for almost thirty years. She never let me down. She was always there when I needed her, even when I didn't *know* I needed her, even though I was a mess for a long time—more years than you've been alive. All that time, I didn't do much besides hurt myself and other people. Your mother was the one I hurt most.

I'm trying to tell you that I know a little about what you've been through. And that I'd like to help, however I can. If you want that help. If you'll accept it.

And that I loved your mother.

26

THREE DAYS LATER, WHEN SHE WAS UP AND ABOUT, we told Alouette that her baby had died and she said, "Yeah, I thought so." She was still on sedation, her eyes dull stones.

I went out that afternoon and bought clothes for her. Jeans and sweatshirts, for the most part, but also a plain cotton dress. That's what she chose to wear when I came by to take her, out on pass, to dinner.

"Well?" she said, standing at half-slouch in the doorway of her room. She had pulled her hair, damaged from months of poor nutrition and utter lack of care, behind her head with a barrette and tried to fluff it out, to give it some body. She wore lipstick that, pale as it was, only emphasized her waxy, sallow complexion. She'd borrowed shoes, navy pumps, from one of the nurses, I guess, along with the lipstick and barrette; I'd bought her a pair of knockoff Nikes.

"*Well*," I said. "Your mother's daughter. No doubt about it."

"Yeah? Well you can be pretty charming for an old fart, even if you are full of shit."

"I'll take that as a compliment."

"Take it any way you want. Where we going?"

"Up to you. Kids still live off pizza?"

"I don't know. Next time I see one, I'll ask."

"I stand corrected, and apologize. How about burgers?"

"How about steaks?"

"That was going to be my very next suggestion."

"Big ones. What time do the gates slam shut on me here, anyway?"

"Ten. So there's plenty of time for a movie too, if you'd like."

"You're pretty ordinary, aren't you, Lewis?"

"I try."

"Okay," she said. We stepped together out of the hospital into a warm fall evening, day's final light fading in a blush of pink and gray just above the trees. "I'll try too."

The place we decided on, with the improbable name of Fred's Steak-Out, looked as though it had slipped through a crack in time from Dodge City or Abilene circa 1860. You could see space between the bare boards of floor and wall, the tables were slabs of wood nailed to lengths of four-by-four and covered with butcher paper and drinks came in old canning jars. The spitoons must have been out back for cleaning. And of course the food was wonderful.

Alouette had prime rib that looked like about half a small cow, a baked potato the size of a football, and mixed greens, mostly kale and collard greens, from the look of it. I ordered grilled tuna with a Caesar salad. We both had iced tea. Lots of iced tea. She still complained of a sore throat from having had the tube in, and thirst from all the drugs.

That night I talked to her more about her mother and me, about our time together. Specific things, things she asked, like had we ever gone here, or done that, and how had it felt when Verne got married and I didn't see her for so long, did it bother me when she was on the streets, what made her decide to give it up finally, how had she managed to do that. We talked, too, about what was going to happen when she got out of the hospital, where she'd go, what her options were (as everybody says these days), and by the time I delivered her back to the hospital, there were glints of light deep within her eyes, stray emotions tugging at the hard lines of her face. Or at least I imagined there were.

Alouette wasn't the only one who needed to check in with reality.

I went back to my room and dialed Chip Landrieu. He'd obviously been asleep.

"Lew Griffin," I said.

There was a long silence.

"It's usually only bad news comes in the night," he finally said.

"Not this time. Look, I'm sorry I haven't been in touch. I'm calling from Memphis, and I've spent the last few weeks down in Mississippi. But I wanted to tell you I've found Alouette."

Another silence. A breath.

"Is she all right?"

"I think so, basically. She's been on some hard drugs, and it's going to be rocky for a while. But I've talked to her a lot these last few days. I think she has a good chance of making it."

I told him about the baby, about Mississippi and my straggling path toward Alouette.

"She'll be getting out of the hospital soon."

"What then?"

"I'm not sure. We've talked about a treatment center up here, or some kind of halfway house. She may want to come back to New Orleans. Right now, it's still one-day-at-a-time time."

"You *will* let me know if there's anything I can do to help, won't you?"

"Absolutely."

"Thanks, Lew. Keep me posted."

"I will."

"You need anything? Money?"

"I'm fine."

"Let me know if you do. Guess I'll owe you a few dozen lunches when you get back."

"You're on."

I sat looking at the phone for a while, finally dialed again but when Clare's answering machine came on the line, hung up.

A minute or two later I called back and told the machine: "It's Lew, Clare. I'm in Memphis. I found Alouette. Sorry I haven't called, but I have been thinking of you."

After hanging up again, I realized that I should have left my number and thought about calling back, but decided to put it off till morning.

I pulled out my notebook and looked up Richard Garces's home number. His machine came on the line, its recorded message in rapid-fire, oddly staccato Spanish, but then Garces himself broke in with "Rick."

I told him who it was and he said, "Hey," stretching it out like a yawn, "good to hear from you."

He'd spoken with Mickey Francis from the hospital and was up to date on pretty much all of it.

"I need some help, Richard. Advice, really."

"You've got it."

"What's Alouette's legal situation?"

"Shaky—as it always is when contentions of mental health are part of the package. Of course in this case there's really no established history of mental health problems, and the girl *is* in her majority."

"If her father doesn't know by now, he will soon enough. I'm expecting lawyers to swoop down on her like a pack of crows."

"I'll have to check to be sure. Laws could be different there; a lot of them are, since everything here is based on the Napoleonic Code. But there's no formal charge as far as the courts are concerned, right? No talk of sanity hearings, anything like that?"

"None."

"That would probably be the way he'd want to go. Claim that the girl was financially dependent, stress her runaway status, abandonment of the baby and its

subsequent death. That's all public record. The lawyers could lean hard on her overdose as a suicide attempt. After that, mostly it would depend on the
judge. Down here, I could pretty much call it according to whose court it was set for. There, I just don't
know. But they'd probably get *some* kind of exclu-
sionary ruling. Commitment to one of the diagnostic
centers for observation, possibly, or mandatory court-
monitored therapy."

"Is there anything we could do to counter it?"

"This isn't science we're talking, Lew. Not even
law, really—and law itself is unpredictable enough.
More like magic where the correspondences are
skewed and whatever rules there are, keep changing.
Let me do some checking. I'll get on the network
and see what I can turn up. I have some contacts
scattered around up there. I'll get back to you. May
be a while. The girl able to sit up straight and say
what *she* wants?"

"Yes. Once she decides."

"She look okay?"

"Yeah. A little shopworn."

"Good. That counts for a lot. Okay, let me fire up
the circuits and read some smoke. Where you gonna
be?"

I gave him my phone number and said if I missed
him, which was likely under the circumstances, I'd
check back with him sometime tomorrow.

I hung up and sat remembering light gouging at
my eyes.

Once years ago, surfacing briefly in a diner during
a week-long drunk, I found Mephistopheles himself
sitting across from me in the booth, pouring Tabasco
sauce into his coffee. At the time it seemed the most
natural thing in the world. We talked a while (I remember the waitress coming by to ask if I needed
anything, and a couple of times to ask if I was all
right, and some other people staring over at us), I de-

clined his offers, and he left, telling me to keep up the good work.

Naturally, I later used the whole thing in a novel.

Tomorrow morning, too, I would call the university, try to mend *that* tattered sail as best I could, if it were mendable at all. Then Clare. Hoping for wind and calm seas.

27

I FOUND HER STANDING AT THE SIDE OF THE TWO-lane highway near a gas-station-and-foodstore crossroad, wearing the cotton dress and navy pumps.

My phone had chirred that morning at eight. Crickets were devouring the Superdome, then there were incoming missiles. The door to my elevator wouldn't close despite a formless something lurking out there in shadow. When my beeper went off, the thing tracking me turned its head suddenly, tipped by the sound—then the sound was only a phone.

Someone's hand went out and got it.

"Mr. Griffin?"

I admitted it.

"Doris Brown, at the hospital. I'm one of the nurses on Three East. We were wondering if you'd seen Alouette."

I came suddenly awake.

"Not since last night. I brought her back about nine-thirty."

"The nurse on duty remembers her coming back, but somehow she never logged back in. And when Trudy made a bed check about two A.M., Alouette was gone." She turned her head away, coughed. "I'm sorry we've been so long getting in touch with you, but we had trouble locating a number for you. You have no idea where Alouette is, then?"

"No."

"Will she contact you, do you think? Or is there someone else she might get in touch with? Her hospi-

talization became voluntary upon release from the jail
ward, of course, but we're concerned.''

"I understand."

"You'll let us know if you hear from her?"

"I will."

I hung up and stood in the shower a long time,
turning the water ever hotter as I adjusted. I'd been
awake much of last night, finally falling into agitated
sleep just as dawn's fingers tugged at the sill. A sleep
in which restless dreams billowed soft and soundless
as silk parachutes and dropped away.

I'd spent those hours preceding my shabby, ragged
symphonie fantastique remembering an incident, itself
almost dreamlike, from years ago.

Every teacher has stories of students who suddenly
give way under pressure. They start coming in during
office hours all the time for no discernible reason, they
just one day vanish and are never seen again, they disrupt class with objections and urgent queries or sit in
the back and never speak, the essays they turn in have
little to do with the subject and everything to do with
themselves.

Oddly enough, in all these on-again, off-again years,
I'd really had only one instance.

The young man's name was Robert. He dressed
neatly, chinos and oxford cloth shirts mostly, and
when he spoke, it was with a demure, softly southern
accent; he had the deferential look of men raised by
women. His French was extraordinarily good. He easily followed everything that was said, evidenced fine
vocabulary and grammar on all written work, but had
trouble whenever things shifted over to speech, as
though words and phrases caught in his throat like
some kind of phlegm and only with great effort could
he expel them.

During conversation one afternoon—we were dis-
cussing Montaigne, as I recall—Robert passed twice,
and when it came around to him again, simply sat

there watching me blankly until I directed a question elsewhere. When I glanced back at him moments later, he leapt from his desk and stood in a crouch beside it.

"*Ça va?*" I asked him.

Whereupon he straightened, announcing in a loud voice, and in perfect French: "There is a conspiracy against me, Mr. Griffin. Surely you know that."

"No, I wasn't aware of that, Robert. But can you tell me just who is involved in this conspiracy?"

He looked around him wildly, but said no more. The room was absolutely quiet. No one moved.

I said: "I'd like for everyone who is not directly involved in this conspiracy to leave the room, please."

The others quickly gathered their things and slipped from the room. I walked over to Robert, who remained standing stock still by the desk.

"So it's down to just us now," he said.

And looking into his eyes, I realized that he wasn't talking to me. I don't think he even knew I was there any longer.

Security came, and Robert let them lead him away without protest. A few weeks later, at a department meeting, Dean Vidale told us that Robert had got up one night at the state hospital, gone into the shower stall, and hung himself with a strip of ticking torn from his mattress.

I was thinking about it again that morning as I climbed back into the car with a huge cup of coffee and a bag of doughnuts and pulled out onto Highway 61. I'm not at all sure why this came to mind. I hadn't thought about it in years. But now that I had, I couldn't seem to shake it.

There was only one place for Alouette to go. And only two reasons for going there, the first of these, and far the least likely, her grandmother.

I'd driven less than an hour, coffee long gone, half a doughnut left in the bag, when, ahead, I saw a semi pull onto the opposite shoulder to let someone off, then pull back into traffic without looking, sending a panicked Camry into the oncoming lane. A panel truck in front of me hit its brakes and swerved onto the shoulder. It fishtailed and came to a stop nose-down in a shallow ditch at roadside, one wheel hanging free. I worked my own brakes, slowing by increments, and at the end of the curve, after the Camry had retaken its lane and shot by me, fell into an easy U.

I watched her face change as I approached and pulled off beside her.

"Thought you might need a ride."

"Guess so. Last one's price was one I didn't want to pay. Man, you get straight and people start *smelling* bad, you know what I mean?"

She got in, crossing her legs beneath her on the car seat.

"He wasn't even going the right direction. I hitched him at a truck stop down the highway and he told me he was bound for Vicksburg. But then we get to the highway and he turns north. And when I say something, he just says, 'What difference does it make, little girl? Places is all alike.'"

"So how'd you persuade him to let you out?"

"I told him I just *couldn't* go back toward Memphis, cause my daddy the sheriff had all-point bulletins out on me up there."

I sat with motor idling. The panel truck backed out, wheels spinning, throwing up dust and stray gravel. A piece flew across the road and banged into the Mazda with a strangely nonmetallic *thunk*.

"Anytime now," she said. "I'm in. We can go."

"Okay. Which way?"

"You mean you didn't come out here to haul me back?"

"Why? You don't want to be there, you'd just leave again. Not much I can do about that. Not much anyone can do about it."

"But me, you mean."

I shrugged.

After a moment I said, "Something I used to do a lot was, I'd line everything up against myself so I had to get slapped back down. Work myself half to death sometimes, just getting it set up that way."

"When you were drinking, you mean?"

"I still drink."

"When you were a drunk, then."

I nodded.

"And you're saying that's what I'm doing."

"No. I'm only saying that I try not to do that anymore. If you want to go back to Clarksville and whatever's there, I'm not going to try to stop you."

"But you came after me."

"Only to talk. You don't want that, we'll shut up, both of us. You don't want to come back up to Memphis, you just open the door and get out. Or you can ask me and I'll drive you to Clarksville myself."

"That's it, that's where I want to go," she said.

"Okay." I waited for a couple of cars to pass, pulled the Mazda back onto the highway and started gaining speed.

"Lewis?" she said.

"Yes."

"You don't preach to me, tell me what's right, what I need to do, like all the rest."

"No."

"Why is that?"

"I figure you know what's right, as much as any of us do. You'll either listen to that, or you won't listen to anything—me, least of all. And you're the only one who can say what you need. Whatever it is, you have to go after that. Everybody does. But needs change, and you don't always notice. Besides," I added, "who'd be fool enough to take advice from me?"

"Let he who is without sin . . ."

I smiled, remembering the last time that came up:

when I was hospitalized for DT's, back when I first met Vicky.

"Something like that. But look who's preaching now."

We rode on in silence.

After a while she said, "Lewis, I think you took a wrong turn back there."

There weren't any turns, only farm roads stretching out like dry tongues to the horizon.

I looked at her.

"Memphis is back that way." She hooked a thumb over her shoulder.

"You sure?"

"I'm sure."

"Memphis it is, then." I pulled off to the shoulder. "And on the way, maybe some lunch?"

"Why thank you, sir," she said in a broad Hollywood-southern accent, "I'd mightily admire to have lunch with a fine, strong man like yourself. One that's paying." She sighed dramatically. "A lady carries no money, you know."

As we rode back, I told her about Bob, how he'd suddenly caved in during class that day.

She sat quietly for a while when I was finished, then said: "Why'd you tell me that?"

"I don't know."

A tractor pulled over to let us pass, rocked back onto the road behind us.

"I think I do."

"I'm listening."

"Because you feel responsible somehow. You think there's something you could have done, that you should have noticed something was wrong. But none of us can be responsible for other people and their lives, Lewis. At your advanced age, you should know that."

She was right.

I should.

I looked over at her, noticing now that her dress
was torn under the arm. Her eyes were amazingly
clear, and she was smiling. I tried to remember if I'd
ever seen her smile before.

28

THE CROWS SWEPT IN THAT NEXT DAY, DROPPING ONTO
us out of a bright, clear sky.

I sat looking out on that day from an alcove tucked
away at the end of the hall. Even the clouds shone with
what seemed their own internal white light.

Two were older, one of them about my age, another
sixtyish with silver hair and eyebrows like frosted
hedges. With them was a lank man in his midtwenties
whose law degree from Tulane had gained him the en-
viable position of carrying their briefcase. He was
dressed like the others in dark three-piece suit and rep
tie, but had a haircut reminiscent of old British films. A
forelock kept falling into his face; he kept brushing it
away with two fingers.

They came off the elevator in V formation and
marched almost in step to the nurses' station, where Eyebrows announced that they were here to see Miss Alouette Guidry, presently going under the name of (he
glanced at Haircut, who fed it to him) McTell.

Jane asked if they were relatives.

"We are attorneys retained by the girl's father to represent her." He made a slight hand motion over his
shoulder and Haircut dealt her a business card.

"Hmmm," Jane said. She picked up the phone, spoke
into it briefly, hung up. "Alouette doesn't wish to see
you," she said.

"I'm afraid that is not satisfactory, young lady."

"Probably not, but unless you gentlemen have further
business, I'll have to ask you to leave."

"What is your name, young lady?"

She pointed to the nametag prominently displayed on her uniform front.

"Then I suppose we must ask to speak with your superior. A supervisor? The physician legally responsible for this unit, perhaps?"

It played out from there, the ball rolling on to a head nurse, an intern and then his resident, and finally to the walleyed young man I'd seen in the administrative offices, who came off the elevator blinking.

"We're here—" Eyebrows began as he disembarked.

"I know why you're here, Mr. Eason."

He patiently explained to them, as had all the others, that Alouette was in her majority; that she, not her father, was the patient here, and the only one whose medical or other needs concerned them at this time; and that, should they wish to pursue the matter, they might best proceed in appropriate fashion through proper channels, as they undoubtedly knew, and *stop* badgering the hospital's employees, taking them away from what could well be urgent duties elsewhere.

"I don't know about Louisiana, gentlemen, but we take our patients' rights seriously here in Tennessee. And now, you *will* please leave."

As though on cue, the elevator doors opened and two security guards stepped off. They stood at either side of the doors as the lawyer trio climbed aboard, then got in with them. The doors shut.

"Jane, let me know at once if there's any further problem," the administrator said, then, turning, saw me sitting in the alcove and came over.

"Mr. Griffin." He held out his hand. I stood, and we shook. "I know about yesterday, of course. We're all rather glad you are here."

"Right now, we're all rather glad *you're* here."

He looked puzzled a moment, then said, "Oh, that. We're used to it. They're serious, or have half a leg to stand on, they've already been to a judge and have paper. Otherwise, it's just a pissing contest.''

"Still, it's appreciated.''

"What I do.''

"Think they'll be back?''

"Up here? No. But we'll be seeing more of them downstairs, I expect. I wouldn't worry about it. Meanwhile, if there's anything I can do to help Alouette, or you, please let me know.''

We shook hands again. He took out a key and pushed it into the control plate beside the elevator doors; within moments, a car was there. He nodded to me as the door closed.

I sat watching pigeons strut along the sill outside, past locked windows. One was an albino, wings and tail so ragged it was hard to believe the bird could still fly.

A moment later Jane answered the phone and said to me, "They're ready, Mr. Griffin.'' I thanked her and walked down the hall to a conference room. Sitting at the table inside were Alouette and Mickey Francis. The social worker held a styrofoam cup, rim well chewed.

"Thanks for coming, Mr. Griffin. Can I get you a cup of coffee?''

"No thanks.''

"I called you to come in because Alouette asked me to. I hope it's not an inconvenience.''

"Not at all. Nothing much going on at the motel this time of day.''

Uncertain whether or not that was a joke, she settled on a smile. Waited two beats. I thought of other such interviews, in rooms much like this one, when I myself was on the home team.

"She and I have talked a lot about what happened yesterday. And over the past several months. I know the two of you have discussed her plans once she's released. Treatment programs, halfway houses, that sort of thing. We all feel it's imperative that she get follow-up care.''

"I think she agrees.''

"She does. And the time for us to shape these decisions is fast approaching."

"Not *us*, Miss Francis. It's her decision all the way."

"You're right, of course." She looked down at the stack of folders on the table before her. "Alouette has expressed to me a desire to go back to New Orleans. Not to remain here."

I nodded. It was home, after all, whatever else it was.

"She would like to find a job, to live independently while participating in an outpatient program."

"Sounds good to me."

"She was wondering if you might be willing to give her a place to live while she did this. She would like to come back to New Orleans with *you*, Mr. Griffin."

I looked at Alouette. She nodded. "Yes, Lewis. That's what I want. If it's all right with you. I know it's a lot to ask."

"You can think about it, Mr. Griffin. You don't have to decide right away. This must come as something of a surprise."

"I'm not much of a role model," I said, "but that house has always been too big for me alone. It would be good to have someone else living there again."

Alouette looked down at the floor a moment, then up at me, smiling. With her mother's eyes.

29

AD HOMINEM TIME.

The following Thursday at nine in the morning, I arrived at the hospital to take Alouette home, stepped off the elevator and found her in conversation with a stately, lean man in blazer, knit shirt and charcoal slacks who, following her eyes, turned and immediately walked toward me. Italian shoes of soft cordovan.

"You must be Griffin," he said, holding out a hand. His shake was firm, relaxed, momentary.

"Lewis, this is my father."

I nodded.

"When I refused to see his lawyers, he canceled everything and flew up himself. He wants to set me up in my own apartment, even has a job arranged for me—no questions, no obligations."

"A generous offer. Not many free lunches left these days."

"I'm sure you'd do the same in my place, Griffin. Do you have children yourself?"

I suspected he knew the answer to that, along with my financial status, personal history and (not inconceivably) the contents of my trash.

And I supposed the answer to his question must be no, so I said that.

Alouette spoke to me over his shoulder: "I told him thanks, but I was going home with you."

"Which I'm certain you must realize is just

not . . . possible," Guidry added, smiling. Between men.

I smiled back.

White teeth gleaming.

Maybe I should break into a chorus of O massuh, how my heart grow weary.

"I see. Then I have to assume you're no more willing to listen to reason than she is."

"It's her decision, Guidry. Not yours, not mine."

"She's a child. A confused child."

"Laws say that she's an adult, and protect her rights the same way they protect yours or mine."

"One has to wonder what *you* expect to get out of this."

"Wonder away."

Instinctively, he had squared off with me. Now he backed away 'a half step. "I know about you, Griffin. You're a weak man. Always have been. One hard push, your knees'll give."

"Push away. Find out."

"A drinker. And inherently a violent man—a killer, some say. That's no environment for a troubled young woman who needs desperately to work out her own problems."

He turned back to Alouette without moving closer.

"I sincerely hope you'll take time to think this whole thing over, come to your senses. See what needs to be done here. I've always taken care of your needs. I always will."

"Needs change," she said with a glance toward me. "Maybe you can't take care of my needs anymore, Daddy."

"And this man can."

"I don't know. Maybe only I can. Or maybe I can't. That's part of what I have to find out."

"I'm telling you here and now that this will *not* happen. I simply can't allow it."

"I've talked to the social workers and hospital lawyers, Daddy. Short of alleging burglary and having me thrown into jail, there doesn't seem to be much you can do about it."

"We'll see about that."

"Do what you think you have to. That's all I'm doing."

"I'll see you both again then—very soon."

He walked to the elevator and stood with his finger on the down button.

"Daddy."

"Yes?"

"There's something I never asked. You always made me feel I couldn't ask it, but I don't feel that way any longer."

He held out an arm to keep the elevator doors from closing. They bucked convulsively. "What is it?"

"Why did you think you had any right to keep me away from my mother?"

He stood looking at her, a squall of emotions ticking at his face in the moment before calm restored itself, then turned and stepped into the elevator.

We spent the next hour extricating Alouette from the hospital's coils. A formal discharge visit from her attending physician; a trip down to the administrative offices where our walleyed champion had prepared the way and we were in and out in minutes, Alouette signing papers to pay off her bill in low biweekly installments; a ride back up to retrieve the clothes I'd bought her and say good-bye to staff and patients.

Then we were walking out into another bright, clear day. Were in the Mazda curving along Riverside Drive. I asked if she wanted to stop for something to eat since there wouldn't be much chance for a while after this, and she said no. She found music on the radio, cranked both that and the seat down low, leaned back and fell promptly asleep. Tunica, Mound Bayou, Cleveland and Greenville rolled over her closed eyes. Hollandale, Redwood. But mostly the same furrowed fields, the same narrow straight roads and blanketing dust, huge spindly irrigation systems linked together like Tinkertoys, little more than hoop wheels and perforated pipe.

Erratic traffic as we approached Vicksburg brought her awake in late afternoon. She opened one eye to peek out the windshield, turned it on me and said hoarsely: "Food?"

Which we partook at a truck stop just off the highway, in accordance with her express desire (when I asked more specifically what she might want) for "food, just food, in large quantities, with lots of grease."

Neither wish was disappointed.

Nor did we fail to attract looks, just looks, also in large quantities, also (for lack of more appropriate synonym) greasy.

It was a place of basics: stand after stand of fuel pumps out front, Spartan restaurant area, cashier's counter with boxes of cheap cigars, pocket knives and belt buckles under its glass top and a rack of T-shirts with clever slogans alongside, bunkerlike bathrooms with rentable showers for truckers.

Clouds had been gathering for some time, bumping up against one another, and as we sat over burned-smelling coffee with oils afloat on its surface, several of them coalesced into one, like a dark fist closing, and rain began pounding at the windows and blacktop outside.

I'd spent those hours on the road thinking of many things.

That, for instance, I'd never got around to calling the university after all.

Or got back to Chip Landrieu.

Or talked to Clare.

Composing in my mind, between Tunica and

Shelby, the second chapter of what was to become *Mole*.

And thinking how, during travel, the mind instinctively shifts mode. Eyes fix on something far off, something unattainable, as you go on about mechanics appearing to have little to do with end or destination: steering, stopping for gas, working pedals; and time itself, unfolding into a plane, a kind of veldt, a portable horizon, all but disappears.

That was also as good a description as any of the life Alouette, and in reflection I myself, would have to live over the coming months.

Perhaps after all, for all our talk of change, redemption or personal growth, for all our dependence on therapists, religious faith or mood-altering drugs both legal and non, we're doomed simply to go on repeating the same patterns over and over in our lives, dressing them up in different clothes like children at play so we can pretend we don't recognize them when we look into mirrors.

After lunch, as we drove on through Vicksburg and veils of rain toward Natchez, Alouette began talking about the hospital. Though barely conscious at the time, she remembered the intubation, fighting against it, to her mind then a worse violation than anything sexual, worse than anything possible.

"But then, suddenly, I broke *free*. Really free. I was floating, drifting, nothing could touch me, nothing could hold me down. I remember thinking: How wonderful this is, I don't even have to breathe now."

Later, pain made its way in, though a pain she could at first easily ignore: therapists drawing blood from her radial artery for ABG's, as she later learned.

"For a long time I was floating just under the surface of things. I could decide whether to come to the top or stay where I was, or at least it *felt* like I had that choice—though I always stayed right there."

But then after a time, half an eternity, the time it

took to rebuild the world, light flooded in. "Light everywhere, so much light that it hurt. God, how it hurt!"

She settled back in her seat and closed her eyes, staring, I suppose, into the face of her own pain and the world's, as I drove on.

We reached New Orleans a little before nine that night.

ACROSS THE STREET NEW APARTMENTS WERE GOING UP. *Broussard General Contractors* had torn down the 140-year-old Greek Revival manse with its rotting ginger-bread, burst columns and disintegrating friezes, left wing for years drooping at an ever steeper angle. Doorways, newels, mantels and windowwork had been stacked in trucks and carted off for resale. Only a few stanchions still stood totemlike near the lot's borders, exposing a once-enclosed central courtyard, the bare heart around which new luxury apartments would be constructed. On the balconies of these apartments in four months, or six, young men and women would stand squinting into the sun, memories watching silently over their shoulders.

We sat outside at steel tables painted yellow and green, under a sky whose sagging bellies of clouds reminded me of the upholstered walls and draped ceilings of old Russia. Every few moments wind puffed its cheeks and Clare put a hand on her napkin to hold it in place.

"I'm sorry, Lew," she said suddenly.

I'd been telling her about Alouette's baby. "It's for the best."

She shook her head. A gesture I'd seen often before, when the wrong words came, or when words wouldn't come at all. "I don't mean that."

I looked back at the clouds, lower now. Something was blowing in across the lake, groping for new ground here.

"I don't know how to say this. I don't even know

what it is I want to say. And I was never good at
speeches—even before.''

A sketchy wave touched at the length of her body,
hinted at the difficult thing her world had become.

''But I won't ever understand it, won't even *begin* to
understand it, if I don't.''

She moved her fork in a gentle sweep through pasta.
There was a *fleur-de-lis* on the plate, and she had pushed
sautéed bits of green pepper into one leaflet of the trefoil,
red into another.

''I never wanted anything to work out more than I
wanted this, Lew. Not that I ever really thought it
would.''

I reached across the table and put my hand over hers.

''Somehow as women we learn to say that all the
time: 'I'm sorry.' As though it's our all-purpose social
formula, good for any occasion, one size fits all. And a
lot of time we're not sorry at all; we don't mean to
apologize, only to say 'I understand' or 'too bad.' But
right now, that's exactly what I mean.''

She looked at me, smiled.

''Where do messages like that come from? How can
we learn to read them so well without even recognizing
that they exist?''

I remembered a poem I'd seen recently in a magazine
at Beaucoup Books: *We must learn to put our distress
signals in code.*

''That's what socialization is, Clare. Most of the messages—maybe all the most important ones—are silent.''

''I guess.''

She took a mouthful of pasta, chewed slowly, sipped
at her wine. Pacing herself, making herself hold back.
Like a runner, or like a hard drinker taking the first one
slow, half convincing himself for the few minutes it lasts
that this is only recreational drinking.

''I think I love him, Lew. I think he loves me. And I
have to do everything I can to give this a chance. Maybe
later on we'll be able to see one another again, if you

want to. But for now . . . It bothers him, Lew. He doesn't
say anything about it, but I can tell. It hurts him, in some
very quiet way he probably doesn't even know or understand himself. But I see it. And I can't do that any
longer."

Clenched about her regret and misgivings, her hand
had become a small fist beneath mine.

"It's okay, Clare."

"No, it's not okay, Lew, not at all. But it's how it
has to be. Do you think we could go now?"

On the way to her car, wind swirling torn paper wrappers and magnolia leaves around our ankles in tides, I
asked how Bat was.

"Gone. I got home last Tuesday and he wasn't there
on top of the refrigerator where he always was. Or anywhere else. I still don't know how he got out. Or why,
for that matter, since he never seemed to have much
interest at all in going out. I waited, thinking he'd show
up again. Last night I finally admitted he wasn't coming
back and put his things away in the pantry, his bowl and
all."

She unlocked the door and I reached around to open
it for her. I told her I was sorry about Bat.

"Life goes on," she said. We kissed and said good-
bye. "I'll call, Lew. When I can."

I watched her drive away, holding my hand up in a
wave as she took the corner onto Joseph. I walked back,
crossed the street and stood for a while in the empty
courtyard, looking across at the restaurant with its yellow and green tables and chairs, its laughing, chattering
people. I imagined the new apartments going up around
me in stop-time, slowly shutting out that world, ma-
rooning me here in this ancient, sequestered place.

31

WHEN I GOT BACK TO THE HOUSE ALOUETTE WAS ON the phone, as she'd been on the phone pretty much non-stop since the morning before. Thus far she had set up two job interviews, attended another, arranged for information to be mailed concerning GED testing and night classes at Delgado, Xavier and UNO, and spoken with an MHMR counselor about vocational programs. Now she was talking to Richard Garces about outpatient therapy and local support groups.

Not long after I came in, she hung up, scribbled one final note and shut the notebook.

"How'd it go?"

I shrugged.

"That bad, huh?"

"Maybe a little worse."

"I'm sorry."

So of course I had to laugh, then explain why.

"Did you know Richard was a hippie? And a junkie? A long time ago, of course."

"It doesn't surprise me."

"Were you a hippie, Lewis? You know, wearing vests without shirts and bell-bottoms and flowers in your hair? Back in the sixties, I mean."

"What I was in the sixties, mostly, was drunk—at least from about '68 on. I didn't pay a lot of attention to social movements. Or to other people, for that matter."

"You were a bodyguard then, right?"

I looked up, surprised. Not many people knew about

that. Verne had, naturally. And Walsh, because that was
how we'd first met.

"I haven't said anything before, but I know quite a
bit about you, Lewis. More than you think."

I poured tea into my cup, added milk.

"When I was in grade school I had this friend, your
classic nerd type, glasses and ugly print shirts, the whole
thing, but he was a computer whiz. What everybody
calls a hacker now. He was really weird. Look, this is
kind of a long story."

"I'll drink slowly."

"And probably a dull one."

"About me? Impossible."

"Yeah, right. Well anyway, Cornell's dad was an en-
gineer with IBM or Apple or someone, and he always
had these new computers around the house, products
they were developing, or marketing. Cornell told me he
grew up with these things as playmates instead of other
kids. He thought everybody did. And he could do anything he wanted with them.

"I was twelve or thirteen. And I just decided one day
that my father couldn't really be my father. Mother was
gone, I was hopelessly miserable. I couldn't talk to him,
or to anyone else in the house, and I knew there was
just no way I belonged there."

"Most children go through that at some point."

"I know that, now. I think I kind of knew it even
then. I was never lucky enough to be stupid."

"But you had to set yourself apart."

She nodded. "And I knew a little about you, just from
things I'd heard. So I decided *you* had to be my father.
It made a lot of sense at the time; it was the only thing
that did. This was about when Cornell and I started being friends. Neither of us had ever had friends before,
and I can't remember now how it happened, but
somehow he started coming over after school, spending
recess and lunch hour with me. One afternoon we
sneaked into this office my father had at home, though

I wasn't ever supposed to be in there, and Cornell showed me how to use the computer. If you knew how, you could dial into all kinds of information banks, he told me; you could find out almost anything you wanted to know.

"I thought about that for days. Then the next Saturday when Cornell came over—my father was at work, as usual—I told him about you. What little I knew, and a lot more I made up. And Monday he brought me this folder full of stuff. Copies of official forms, printouts of what I guess had been newspaper articles, parts of some kind of dossier the FBI had on you. That one said you killed a man."

I nodded.

"A sniper, according to the dossier. It said he'd killed at least eight people."

"At least."

"You stopped working as a bodyguard after that."

"I stopped doing much of anything. Just kind of drifted into it. Drank a lot. It was a bad time."

"Every night I'd get out that folder and read it. It was like making constellations out of stars: just raw information, that you could fill out any way you wanted. So every night I'd look at some facts, facts I knew by heart by then, and use them to make up stories about you. Those stories became more real to me than the world around me, more real than anything else, and for a time, far more important. Though all along I knew it wasn't true. I knew you weren't my father."

"And that I wasn't a hero."

She nodded. "And that life is just doing the things you have to do: staying alive, getting through the day, turning into your parents. Maybe I was wrong about that part, huh? Maybe there's something more to it?"

"Maybe."

"Can I make you another pot of tea? That has to be cold by now."

"Only if you'll have some too. I'm already sloshing when I walk."

"Deal."

We went out to the kitchen. I leaned against the sink thinking of meals I'd prepared long ago for Verne, for Vicky and Cherie, remembering their laughter, seeing their faces, as Alouette emptied the kettle, drew fresh water and put it on to boil, filled the pot with hot water from the tap.

"Transportation's going to be the biggest problem," she said. "I figure between work, group meetings and whatever classes I settle on, I'm going to be piling up a lot of miles. I'll centralize what I can, find locations closer in to home. But some of it, like work and school, won't be so easy."

"Give it time. We'll see. Things start working out so that you decide you need a car, I'll match whatever money you can save up for one. And I'll take you to a friend who has a used-car lot and owes me a few favors."

"All *right*."

She emptied the pot, measured in Earl Grey, poured water, stirred once and set it to steep under a brocade cozy Vicky had sent me from Scotland years back.

When the tea was ready, we went back into the living room. Alouette settled on the couch with her notebook, feet tucked under her. I sat in my chair with a copy of Queneau's *Zazie dans le métro*. I looked up at her after a while and thought how strange this tableau, this quiet domestic scene, was for both of us. Then how very alone I had been all these years, and how good it was to have someone here again.

QUENEAU ONCE REMARKED THAT JUST ABOUT ANYONE could learn to move characters around, getting them from place to place and scene to situation, pushing them through pages like sheep until finally one arrived at something people would read as a novel. But Queneau himself wanted the characters and their relationships—to one another, to the sprawl of human history and thought, to the book itself—to be structured, wanted those relationships to be in the word's purest sense *constructed*: in short, he wanted something more.

There are those who would argue—*engagés* like Sartre, or perhaps in our own country the late John Gardner—that, in eschewing the tenets of "realistic" or mimetic fiction, he wanted less.

This strain of what we might call irrealism, this motive of artifice, in French fiction reaches back at least to Roussel, whose *Locus Solus* some of you may have encountered in Jack Palangian's magic-realism seminar, and persists today in the work of Georges Perec, the group OuLiPo—cofounded by Queneau, incidentally—and American expatriate Harry Mathews.

Le Chiendent, Queneau's first published novel, in fact consciously, deliberately parodies most all the conventions of realistic fiction.

It is a rigorously structured novel. Ninety-one parts: seven chapters each containing thirteen sections, each of them with its three unities of time, place and action, each confined to a specific mode of representation, or narrative: narration only, narration with dialogue, dialogue alone, interior monologue, letters, newspaper articles, dreams.

The novel, a meditation on the Cartesian *cogito*, in fact had its beginning in Queneau's attempt to translate Descartes into demotic French. It opens with a bank clerk, Étienne Marcel, coming to consciousness, surfacing out of the slough of his unexamined life, while looking into a shop window. Taking substance from his sudden self-consciousness, *and* from the objective existence accrued from Pierre le Grand, who has happened to see him there at the window and become curious about him, Étienne is plunged headlong into a series of adventures—into the thick of life itself.

At one point le Grand, through whose eyes we witness much of the book's early action, says: "I am observing a man." And his confidante replies: "You don't say! Are you a novelist?" To which he replies: "No. A character."

As things go on, and as still more characters and situations are introduced, many of them truly bizarre—it's rather like those jugglers who begin with a small cane or club and end up piling chair atop chair, all of it tottering there far above them—the novel turns ever more fantastic, drifting further and further from the moorings of realistic fiction, until at last the reader is forced to abandon any pretense that he's reading a story about "real" people or events and to admit that he is only participating in the arbitrary constructions—reflective, complex, but always arbitrary—of a writer. A sophisticated game-playing.

From one of the novel's many discursive passages:

"People think they are doing one thing, and then they do another. They think they are making a pair of scissors, but they have made something quite different. Of course, it is a pair of scissors, it is made to cut and it cuts, but it is also something quite different."

A character muses: Wouldn't it be wonderful to be able to say what that "something else" is? And that is exactly what Queneau attempts, here and in all his work: to touch on that "something else" we sense, yet never locate, in our lives.

Yet because he has a kind of horror of seriousness, it's often at their most profound moments that his books and poems turn outrageously comic, dissolving into puns, bits of allusive and other business, vaudeville jokes, slapstick. One often thinks they are books that might have been written by an extraordinarily brilliant child.

Which brings us, quite naturally, to *Zazie,* a best-seller for Queneau and perhaps his most easily accessible novel.

As the book opens, murderous dwarf Bébé Overall has abducted little Zazie from the department store where her young mother was choosing fine Irish linen and has taken her into his underground lair far beneath the Paris *métro* lines, a place frequented by old circus performers, arthritic guitar players and legless Apache dancers, ancient socialists with Marx-like beards and tiny Trotsky spectacles. There Bébé—

Yes, Miss Mara?

I see. You may be right; perhaps in my enthusiasm I am not describing Queneau's novel at all, but rather some alternate version, some *possibility*, of my own; have begun, as some colleagues might say, deconstructing it. Why don't *you* tell us what *actually* happens in *Zazie dans le métro?*

33

I WAS, IN A SENSE, SINGING FOR MY SUPPER. A LATTER-day minstrel show for ol' massuh, ol' massuh in this case being Dean Treadwell, who had chosen today—my first day back, after yesterday sheepishly calling my department chairman, apologizing for my absence so profusely that I began to stammer, and finally pleading a family emergency—to audit, as was his custom once each term with every course offered under his aegis, my class.

Miss Mara acquitted herself well, the students had actually read *Zazie,* and discussion was lively. One of the young men took a particular, keen delight in Zazie's Uncle Gabriel, pitching his voice throughout the discussion in a high, thin flutter he obviously imagined similar to the uncle's own during his performances as a female impersonator.

As the students filed out, Dean Treadwell came up to me and held out his hand.

"Fine class. Somehow you have a way of making it all real to them, making them care. I wish half of my other teachers could do that."

"You caught me on a good day. Most others, the snoring would have distracted you."

"Fascinating. And I never even *heard* of Queneau before this."

"Three weeks ago, none of the students had either. A semester from now, most of them will have forgotten him."

"You have a minute, Lew?"

"Actually, I have about four hours—till my seminar after lunch."

"Walk with me, then. I'll buy you a coffee."

"Sure. But if the coffee's from one of the faculty lounges, I'll pay *you* not to have to drink it."

We ambled out into the hallway and along it, heads together like two monks strolling the cloisters as they kicked Boethius back and forth.

"I don't know how you'll feel about this . . ."

I let it hang there.

"I understand from some of the faculty members, and from my wife as well, that you worked for many years as a detective."

"Worked *at* it, anyway."

Two of my students from Advanced Conversational passed us. One of them said *Bonjour*, the other Hey, how's it going?

We wound up off-campus, at one of the coffeehouses that suddenly seem to be springing up everywhere in New Orleans. This one was a Tennessee Williams set: a hodgepodge of rickety ancient tables and chairs, crumbling plaster walls, windows so hazed you could safely watch eclipses through them, door open onto a dank inner patio where a three-legged cat furiously eyed all trespassers. A massive mahogany counter built directly into the tiled floor and topped with a slab of green marble dominated the room. A cork bulletin board took up most of the back wall, scaled in layers of handbills for alternative music, scribbled ads offering musical equipment for sale, notices of tutors and roommates wanted.

Like many such places in the city, it was a museum exhibit in other ways as well: here, an unregenerate hippie in jeans, work shirt and vest, scraggly hair stuffed into a bandanna; a fifties young professional in polyester "smart" frock and bouffant hair, or facsimile beatnik with goatee, shades and beret; over there, a black man natted out in suit and impossibly wide tie dating from the forties, slicked hair close to his scalp under a wool

slouch hat. People have a way of getting stuck in time
here in New Orleans. Once a student fresh from New
Hampshire asked "Are all these strange-looking people
here for Mardi Gras?" and another student told her,
"Those are the ones who live here."

"Why did you give it up?" Treadwell asked me when
we were seated over tall, untouchably hot glasses of *café
latte.* "Detective work, I mean."

"I'd tell you I found honest work instead, but you
know better."

He laughed silently, a single brief paroxysm, and
looked off toward the patio. Sitting in the doorway with
its stump raised for cleaning, the cat glared back at him.

"You've been married, haven't you, Lewis?"

"Once, a long time ago."

"And you had children?"

"I did. A son. He's gone now."

Treadwell's eyes came back to me.

"Gone?"

I shrugged. "It doesn't matter. But all this has to be
leading up to something."

"I was married once, when I was younger than seems
possible now. It didn't last long, and afterward, I was
by myself for a long time, one of those academic bachelors who comes out of the house on his way to classes
slapping dust and crumbs off his coat. I never imagined
I'd live any other way. But—What's the old saying?
life's all conjunctions, just one thing after another?"

"More like punctuation, I think. Colons and excla-
mations for some, dashes for the rest."

"One day in Victorian Life I looked up from my notes
and, I still don't know why, noticed a young woman
sitting there in the front row. Older than the other students, but still young to me. And while I was looking,
while the fact of her existence was slowly sinking in as
I prattled on about the monarchy or somesuch, she
winked at me. Not coquettishly at all, you understand,
but with this amazing sense of maturity somehow, of

being very much her own person . . . solid.

"I dismissed class shortly thereafter. That was on a Thursday. And by Monday we were married. Twelve years ago. Twelve years. From the first I felt as though I'd packed up everything and moved to a new country. A different language, different customs, different weather—who knows, maybe even different physical laws. *Everything* changed."

I waited. Good interviewers never have to say much; they turn themselves into voids, into receptacles.

"Laura *is* my life now, everything else revolves around her, her and the university. But I have a son by that first, youthful marriage. He's an adult himself now, of course. We never had much to do with one another, never communicated much; he grew up on the West Coast, mostly. But a couple of months ago he moved back here, to New Orleans, and we began seeing one another. He'd call every week or so. We'd meet for lunch, a glass of wine. It's an ambiguous relationship, at best. Would you like more coffee?"

I declined, and after a moment he said, "I'm afraid he's in trouble. I wondered if you might be able to help him." Then he added: "Laura's dead against my getting involved."

This is none of your business, Griffin echoed far back in my head. I said: "I'd have to know two things. What kind of trouble—"

"Drugs. I don't know how deeply."

"Then your wife may be right. The other thing I'd have to know is what you'd expect me to do. There's probably not much you, or I, or anyone else *can* do. You have to know that."

He nodded, head remaining momentarily bowed. "I suppose in a sense I've dedicated my life to the belief that knowledge, that learning, intellect, reason, *matter*." He looked back up. "Yes, I know. I've dealt with this in my usual manner: I settled into the library and read everything available. But now I seem to be flying in the face of all that, don't I?''

"If not flying, at least taking one hell of a leap of faith.''

"Too close to the son,'' he said. I wouldn't have thought he had it in him.

And because of that, as much as anything else, I told him I would do it.

I got the son's address, a snapshot (his only one, he told me as he pulled it from his wallet) and as many details of his son's life as he knew. There weren't many: a workplace that might or might not be current, a bar he'd mentioned a couple of times, a few friends' first names. His son drove an old mustard-color Volvo, loved spicy food and war movies, was not a reader and had no particular taste for music.

"I want to know how bad it is,'' Dean Treadwell said, "how deeply he's into this. That's all I expect of you. Maybe then I can find a way to help him.''

"I'll do what I can. I still have a few contacts out there. I'll ask around, turn over some stones.''

Treadwell had pulled a checkbook out of his coat pocket and was uncapping a pen.

I shook my head. "This is a favor. Besides, it may well come to nothing.''

"I insist.''

"So do I.''

"Very well, then.'' He clipped pen to checkbook and slipped them back into his pocket. "At least promise that you'll come over for a meal with Laura and me, soon.''

"I'll be in touch.''

Outside, he turned back.

"Lew. I almost forgot: my wife made me promise to ask when there's going to be a new book. She's read them all, and said to tell you she loves them, especially the ones set in New Orleans.''

"Tell her thanks, but I'm not sure. Lately I seem to be getting distracted by life a lot.''

Neither of us knew, of course, that the next book when it came, written in a two-week binge of twenty-hour days and published just before *Mole*, would be the story of his own son's last days.

IT WAS MUCH WORSE THAN HE SAID, OF COURSE. PROBably even worse than he thought.

The first thing I did that afternoon, from my airless, shared office in the basement of Monroe Hall, was call Walsh. They couldn't find him for a while, and I sat listening to a rumble of shouts and clatter, indecipherable conversations, other phones buzzing. Finally he came on with "Yeah?"

"Lew."

"Listen, I don't care how much you beg, I'm not buying you any more dinners."

"Two desirable bachelors like us, both our calendars are probably filled anyway, bubba."

"Well, I might just be able to squeeze you in—but you'd have to buy."

"I'm not that desperate yet."

"You will be."

"So I'll call you back when I am."

"Sure you will." Someone spoke to him, and he turned away briefly, came back. "How's the girl?"

"Doing okay, this far."

"Good sign. Any word from Clare?" When I said nothing, he went on. "Yeah, well, I'm sorry about that, Lew, I really am."

"Life goes on."

"Yeah. Such as it is. So what kind of favor you need this time? Not a big one, I hope. The city just dumped a new load of shit on us and now the mayor and his boys are down here smearing it all around."

I told him.

"You at home?"

"School." I gave him the number.

Twenty minutes later, he called back.

"What about the mayor and his boys?" I asked.

"Hey, urgent police business came up. It happens like that. They're cooling their buns on the bench out in the squad room, staring at me in here. Told them I'd be right out, soon as I took care of this emergency. First time I've sat down today."

"Maybe I should thank them."

"Maybe you should shoot the whole lot of them."

"So what's the story?"

"Well, it looks like your boy's cut himself a little swath down the coast from Seattle to Portland."

"Drugs?"

"Initially. Possession, PI, sales. Then your man went to school somewhere: suddenly B&E, suspicion of auto theft and attempted fraud start rolling up. No convictions on any of it, so a lot of this isn't on the record, but he became a familiar face. A couple of short falls, one for assault and battery, the other for, get this, unpaid traffic tickets. He's been lucky. But the captain I talked to up there said he's a body ready to drop. That help?"

"You bet. Thanks, Don."

"You want me to keep the net open on this?"

"No. Good enough."

"This guy's in town, I take it."

"Yeah."

"Yet another fine example of scuz rising to the bottom. I'm sure he'll be in to say hello sooner or later."

"Good chance of it."

"So I have to go feed the lions now, right?"

"Guess so. Pull a tail for me."

"You got it."

I could have just called Dean Treadwell then, of course. It was what he wanted to know—more than he wanted to know. My favor was done. But I didn't want to break the old man's heart, I told myself, not in such an impersonal fashion.

If you're in New Orleans with time to kill and a taste for alcohol, sooner or later you run into Doo-Wop. And sooner or later you'll probably buy him a drink and get into a conversation with him.

Every day Doo-Wop makes his steady round of bars from the Quarter up through the Irish Channel and along Oak Street. That's what he *does*, that's his job, and he pursues it with single-minded devotion. And because after all this time he's as much part of the city landscape as palm trees or the buildings along St. Charles, he gets free drinks, a lot of them from the bartenders themselves, a lot from bar regulars, some from drop-in drinkers. Anybody who buys Doo-Wop a drink buys a conversation too.

And if you ever had one of those conversations, Doo-Wop remembers it. He can't remember if he ever had another name or where he's from, he doesn't know the year or who the president is and probably can't tell you where he stayed last night, but if you talked to him, last week, last month, or back in the summer of '68, Doo-Wop's still got it all.

I found him after a couple of hours, in the twelfth or fourteenth place I tried. He was seated on a stool at the bar, drinking tequila since that's what the guy buying was drinking, and talking about his days as a Navy SEAL. I doubt he was ever a SEAL, but he'd probably spent a few hours with one sometime in a bar much like this one. That's what he did with all that conversation, why he collected all those stories. They were his stock in trade, the product he traded for drinks and companionship of a sort.

"Big guy," he said as I came in, looking into a mirror so silvered that it turned the whole world into an antique photograph. "Long time." He was wearing high-top black tennis shoes laced halfway up, a purplish gabardine suit, plaid sport shirt with thin black tie.

"Too long." I signaled the barkeep, who shuffled over and simply stared at me till I said, "Two more tequilas for these gentlemen and whatever's on draft for me."

"No draft."

"An Abita, then."

"No Abita."

"Dixie?"

He nodded and shuffled toward the bend in the bar, sliding his feet along stiffly as though on skis.

"Big guy, this's . . ."

We both waited a moment.

"Newman," his companion said.

"From Missoula, Montana." Doo-Wop hurriedly threw back what remained of his old drink before the new one got there. He didn't like things in life getting ahead of him. "Has him a little ranch up there, breeds horses." He nodded toward Newman in the mirror. "Next time we run into each other, remind me to tell you about that Arabian stable I worked at down in Waco."

Since he'd finished the drink Newman bought him, the subtle morality of Doo-Wop's enterprise allowed him now to cut Newman loose in my favor, and he motioned toward a booth in one corner. We waited at the bar for our drinks, then settled in there.

"So what's up, big guy? Who you looking for?"

"How do you know I'm looking for someone?"

"Big guy. You ever come see me just to have a quiet drink? You got your business, I got mine, right? And sometimes they kind of fetch up against one another. Way the world works. Damn glass empty again."

I motioned for the barkeep to refill it and showed Doo-Wop the snapshot Dean Treadwell had given me.

"Twice. Once at the Cajun Bar on Tulane, the other time over on Magazine, the Greek's place."

It wouldn't do any good to ask when; time didn't exist for Doo-Wop.

"From Washington. Near Seattle, he said. Did a stretch or two up there. Not very interesting. Didn't have any stories that amounted to anything, didn't pay much attention to mine."

"I don't suppose he wrote his address on a matchbook and gave it to you?"

"Not as I recall."

"That was a joke, Doo-Wop."

He thought about it a minute. "Never did quite get the hang of that joke thing."

"What I meant was, did he happen to say anything about where he was staying."

"Not a word. Said he had a couple of things going. Usually means a man's right next to eating rats off the street."

"Okay. Thanks, guy. You see him again, and remember to, you call me?" I laid a ten-dollar bill and a business card on the table.

He picked up the bill, leaving the card. "I already got one of those from last time."

I stood to leave, Doo-Wop to move back to the bar.

"Ask the Greek," he said. "Guy did some work for him. Heard that, anyway."

I got a twenty out of my wallet and handed it to him. He stuck it down in his shoe with the other bill.

"You come have a drink with me sometime when it ain't business. I'll buy," he said. "You know where to find me."

35

THE GREEK WASN'T GREEK, BUT PUERTO RICAN. HE *was* from a foreign country—New York—and wore the sort of bushy, untrimmed mustache often seen on Mediterranean males. His name was Salas, which upon his arrival in New Orleans had sounded to someone enough like the Greek surname Salus to earn the sobriquet he'd had ever since. He'd worked as *maître d'* for years at restaurants from Kolb's to Upperline before a heart attack dropped him flat into a client's swordfish steak with béarnaise at age twenty-nine. Coming out of the hospital, he's simplified his life: got rid of most of what he owned, bought this place, a decaying, abandoned corner grocery store on Magazine with Spartan apartment above, and turned it into a neighborhood bar, a remarkably laid-back, low-key one, even for New Orleans. He served some of the best gumbo and sandwiches in town, if you didn't mind waiting a while.

The weekend after papers were signed, an army of uncles, brothers and cousins had appeared from nowhere and set about shoring the place up. It was as though they converged on a derelict grocery store, swarmed briefly and stepped back from a bar; and not much had changed since. The beams and supports they'd fashioned from two-by-twos, still bare wood but now gone green with mildew and mold, still propped up corners and ceiling. Cracks in the plaster troweled over with little or no effort to match the color of new plaster to old now looked like skin grafts long since rejected.

Living in a third-floor apartment across the street at

the time, with nothing much to do on weekends till seven o'clock rolled over and I allowed myself to begin the night's drinking, I'd watched the whole thing. The Greek's was on my parade route, the place I started and more often than not ended my nights. It was also one of the few bars in the city I'd never been thrown out of. There had been a name on the window at one point, but no one ever paid any attention to it, and when the name faded away, it was never replaced.

Carlos was sitting on a footstool behind the bar, one hand gently swirling ice around the bottom of what remained of a glass of lemonade, the other holding open a paperback book. I might have been gone twenty minutes, instead of twenty years.

Carlos wanted to know about me, so I gave him a two-minute version. I asked the same in return, and he shrugged and moved his head to indicate the bar.

"Get you a drink?"

"Not today, Carlos, I'm in a hurry. Let me come back when I have more time."

He smiled and nodded, waiting for me to say what I'd come for.

I showed him the snapshot of Treadwell's son. "He been around?"

"Last I heard, you'd quit doing detective work."

"I have. This is more like a favor. You know him?"

"Teaching, I heard. Always thought that was something I'd be good at, if things had turned out a lot different."

"The picture, Carlos."

"He in trouble?"

"Not yet."

"But he's planning something."

"I don't know if he's planning it or not, but he's about to break an old man's heart."

"Old man?"

"His father."

Carlos shook his head. "That's bad. What can I tell you?"

"Where he's staying would be a good start."

"Couple weeks ago, he was staying with a guy named Tito, over on Baronne a block off Louisiana. I don't know if he's still there. Or the address, but it's this huge blue monster, textured plaster, at the edge of an open lot. Tito's place is upstairs on the left. There's a separate staircase up to it."

"This Tito a salesman?"

"So they say."

"And a relative of yours, by any chance?"

"A cousin, as it happens. Tito's never there in the afternoon. That would be a good time for you to drop by."

"Then that's what I'll do."

I thanked him and said I'd see him soon, looking at the clock over the bar as I left. Almost five. My seminar students had walked long since. But it was still afternoon, at least.

I caught a cab at Jackson Avenue, had the driver take me up St. Charles to Louisiana and got out there. Walked two blocks to Baronne. I saw the building as soon as I turned.

It was a shade of blue not found in the natural world. The texturing on its plaster sides reminded me of Maori masks. Two cars and a pickup truck were stacked up in the driveway alongside like planes waiting for takeoff clearance, but they'd been waiting a long time.

The railing at the top of the stairs was hung with towels and a washcloth, an orange cotton rug, a shirt on a hanger. I knocked at the screen door, waited a moment, then opened it and knocked on the glass of the door inside. When there was still no response, either from within or from curious neighbors, I pulled out an old plastic ID card I keep for this very purpose and slipped the lock.

The door opened directly into the kitchen. A quarter

inch of leftover coffee baked to black tar on the bottom
of its carafe. Grease half filled the gutters around the
stove's burners. The whole apartment smelled of cat,
equal parts musk and pee, with the heady, sweet reek of
marijuana beneath. Furnishings were minimal, cast-off
clothes in abundance.

I found some Baggies of grass and crack stashed
among provisions—mostly unopened jars of spices,
sacks of flour, sugar and baking soda, and canned goods
like corned-beef hash and stew—and put them back. I
found a .38 under the cushion of one of the chairs in the
living room and put that back too.

Off to one side was a windowless, odd-shaped little
room of the sort often seen in these huge old places that
have been chopped into apartments again and again. A
mattress had been crammed into it. One corner was bent
back like a dog-eared page where the room took a sudden turn; an edge lapped over the baseboard. A nylon
athletic bag lying on the mattress had been used as a
pillow. I opened it and found in a manila envelope
stuffed with scraps and folds of paper an expired Washington driver's license issued to Marcus Treadwell. Most
of the rest was people's names and addresses, with notations in a tiny, precise script, in what I presumed to
be a code.

I stepped back into the living room and discovered
that the .38 was no longer under the cushion. It was now
in someone's hand, and pointed at me.

"You must be Tito."

He nodded.

"I'm a friend of Carlos."

"Carlos don't live here, man."

"I know. I was just down at the bar talking to him.
He thought you might be able to help me."

"What you need help with?"

"I'm looking for something."

"Just something for yourself? You don't look like a

user, man. And I don't do wholesale, know what I mean?''

I shook my head. ''Not drugs.''

''I'm willing to believe that.''

''The guy who's been sleeping here.''

''What you want with that pile of shit?''

''Just to talk.''

''Yeah? Well, you find him, I want to talk to him too, but I won't be talking long.''

''Guess you guys didn't hit it off.''

''Hey, I thought he was okay, you know? Till I come home yesterday morning and find him with the back of the crapper off, going after my stash. I'd already moved it, but that don't matter. But I guess he heard me coming, 'cause he was out the window and gone in about half a second. Wouldn't have thought the boy could move that fast.''

''You saw him?''

He shrugged. ''Who else would it be?''

''Listen, are you going to shoot me or not? Cause if you're not, I'm going to reach into my pocket for a picture.''

''Nah, man, I ain't gonna shoot no one.'' He stuck the gun in a back pocket.

''This the guy?''

''Yeah.''

''And you haven't seen him since yesterday morning?''

''No.''

''What time?''

''Nine, ten, something like that. He try to rip you off too?''

I shook my head.

''You got a message for him, that right?'' Tito said.

''More or less.'' I handed him a card. ''If you do see him again, think about giving me a call.''

''There money in it?''

"You never know. For now, let's just say it will be much appreciated."

He looked at the card, then up at me. "Lew Griffin. I heard of you. People say you used to be bad."

"I used to be a lot of things."

"Yeah. Know what you mean."

"I might drop by again tomorrow or the next day, just to check, if that's okay."

"Sure. You do that, Lew Griffin. Just don't forget to lock up again when you leave."

He grinned, gold bicuspid flashing. I suddenly remembered that my father had one just like it.

36

WALSH AND RICHARD GARCES WERE COMING FOR DINner that night. I'd done most of it ahead, a cassoulet and flan, and Alouette was in charge of the rest. When I stepped through the door at seven-twenty I found them all sitting together in the living room. Richard had a glass of wine, Walsh a tumbler of bourbon, Alouette one of those prepackaged wine cooler things. No one got up, but three faces swiveled toward me.

"There goes the party," Garces said.

"And the neighborhood." Alouette.

"Buck seems to be stopping here." Walsh.

"What would you like, Lewis?" Alouette again. I followed her out to the kitchen, pulled an Abita out of the fridge. The kitchen was warm and full of wonderful smells.

"Everything set?"

"Cassoulet's heating, bread's in the oven with it, salad's made except for the dressing."

"You've been watching reruns of Donna Reed."

"Who?"

"Never mind. Anything I can do?"

"Go sit down, drink your beer and talk to the guys. I'll throw this stuff together."

"You sure?"

"Shoo."

It had felt good being in the kitchen again last night, preparing for this, and it felt good now sitting with friends, talking about nothing in particular, anticipating more of the same. I laid my head back, felt tensions go out of my body. My mind rippled with stray thoughts, then became still water.

"Had a call from a friend of yours today," Walsh said. "Sergeant Travis up in Mississippi. Asked how things were going down here. And wanted me to tell you things are a lot duller there now that you're gone."

"I hope you don't mind," Garces said, "but I've asked Alouette to see *Torch Song Trilogy* with me this weekend; they're doing it at the Marigny. It's sold out— which means about twenty tickets—but I have friends in unimportant places. It's Saturday night. That's all right?"

"Sure. Do her good to get out. She's become kind of monomaniacal about this whole thing."

"She has to, for a while."

"I know."

"She seems to be doing well. I have a good feeling about it."

Moments later, Alouette called us to table. We all went out to the kitchen to help her bring things in, forming a culinary chorus line on our way back through the open double door, me with cassoulet, Richard with salad and a huge basket of bread, Don with a tray of condiments and a pitcher of iced tea, Alouette with serving spoons, trivet and a pot of coffee.

The usual dinnertime conversation—politics, jokes, anecdotes, compliments—mixed with grunts of satisfaction and the clatter of silverware. The coffee disappeared fast, and before long I went out to the kitchen to make another pot. When I came back, Alouette was saying: "I can't plan too much ahead. I mean, I want to, but I know I just can't do that, that it doesn't make sense."

"You're right," Richard said. "That's part of what addiction's all about. The personality type, anyway. You start setting up a scene in your head for how things *should be,* and before long you'll look at what's there and how far it is from what you envisioned, from your expectations—and fall into the gap."

" 'I fear those big words that make us so unhappy,' "
I said.

Everyone looked at me.

"James Joyce."

"We . . . *fear* . . . change," Alouette said.

"*Wayne's World.*" Garces. We were an allusive, cultured bunch.

Walsh asked about Treadwell then, and I filled him in.

"Your dean's going to have his face rubbed in shit, any way you look at it, Lew. He ready for that?"

"Hard to say. At some level or another, he probably already knows. I think he wants me to be able to tell him everything's all right. But I also think he knows that's not going to happen."

We sat around the table long after dinner and the second pot of coffee were finished. I'd put music on low, a Yazoo anthology of early jazz guitar including the Eddie Lang-Lonnie Johnson duets (for which Lang had used an assumed name, since black and white musicians didn't record together in those days), and a recent CD by New Orleans banjoist Danny Barker.

Walsh bailed out, bleary-eyed, about eleven, Garces within the hour. In each case I threw my arms across the door and explained that they had to take cassoulet with them or would not be allowed to leave. As usual, the cassoulet had gone upscale from a small skillet to the kitchen's largest ovenworthy vessel.

Alouette and I for a while made motions toward cleaning up, mostly just picking things up in one place and putting them down somewhere else. Finally we abandoned pretense and sat at the kitchen table to finish off the iced tea. Out in the front room Danny Barker was making his third or fourth trip of the night down to St. James Infirmary.

I started telling her about David, how I hadn't been around when he was growing up, how we'd at last got to know one another a little, not really as father and son (though I guessed those feelings were there) but more as two adults living in very different worlds.

"He'd gone to Europe for the summer, and sent a postcard or two. Bored gargoyles on one of them, I remember. But we had this pattern—nothing at all for months, then one of us would write a ten-page letter—so I didn't think anything of it. But then his mother called to say she hadn't heard from him either and couldn't seem to get in touch with him."

Alouette listened silently.

"I started trying to find him, figuring there'd be nothing to it. He was in Paris. Apparently he boarded a flight to return to the States, and a cabdriver thought he remembered picking him up at Kennedy and letting him off near Port Authority. But then it was as if he'd dropped off the edge of the earth. There was no trace of him, whatever I did.

"Once about this time, someone called me and said nothing but stayed on the line until the answering machine automatically broke the connection. And somehow, for no good reason, with no idea why he might call like that, or why he wouldn't speak, I knew it was David."

I didn't tell her that, like one of Beckett's mad fabulists, I still had the tape with that silence on it.

Alouette waited, and when she was certain I was through, said: "You never found him, or found out what happened?"

"Nothing."

She reached across the table and laid her hand loosely on mine. "I'm sorry, Lewis. It must hurt terribly."

"It should. But what it really feels like, is that the hole in me, the one that's always been there, just got bigger. And now I know it won't ever be filled."

I removed my hand to pat hers briefly and retrieve my tea. "Well. That last beer seems to have carried me right past philosophical and poetic drunk straight to maudlin."

"*In vino veritas.*"

"I never found any. And God knows I spent enough years looking. Right now—I've been giving this some thought—I've decided that I may have just enough energy left to crawl up the stairs to my room."

We walked up together, and at the head Alouette turned back.

"Why did you tell me about David, Lewis?"

Because it's the deepest, most guarded thing in me that I have to give you, I thought.

"I don't know," I said.

37

I SPENT MOST OF THE NEXT DAY CHASING SNIPE. No one in any bar in New Orleans had ever seen anyone remotely resembling Treadwell's son. Most of them couldn't even be bothered to look at the snapshot. He had not registered at any of the employment services, applied for a driver's license or library card (how's that for desperation?), rented storage space or a postal box from one of the private facilities. No parking tickets had been issued to any vehicle registered in his name. Local credit and collection agencies had received no inquiries.

At four that afternoon I was sitting in a coffeehouse on Magazine, Rue de la Course, gulping my second large *café au lait* from a glass and watching downtown workers bolt for an early start out of the CBD. Nineteenth-century testimonials to the social position and restorative powers of coffeehouses, hand-lettered, hung on the wall at eye level, at least a dozen of them, most with cheap frames askew. It had been some time since anyone took note of them.

Because I could think of nothing else to do, yet remained more or less in function mode, I called Tito, and was surprised when he picked up.

"Hey," he said. "I was gonna call you and couldn't find that card you gave me. It's here somewhere. Cause I heard from the guy you were asking about. Told me he got picked up in the Quarter a few nights ago and he's been in jail all this time, so I guess it wasn't him that tried to rip me off after all. You still got a message

for him, I wanted you to know he says he's getting out
in the morning.''

"You be there a while?''

"What for?''

"Thought I might bring by some solid appreciation.''

"Hey. It's a favor, man. Like I say, I heard about
you. And besides, it's the second week of the month.
Got to go see my parole officer. Cute little thing. Always
got a bow in her hair, different one each time. Great ass,
for a white girl.''

"Has a lot of good advice for you, I bet.''

"*Deep* conversations. *She* know what it like here, no
doubt about it.''

"Tito: thanks, man.''

"Just don't forget, Lew Griffin. Next time, maybe *I'm*
the one needs a favor, who knows. Happens.''

"It does indeed.''

I walked to Prytania, got a cab and gave the driver
my home address. Halfway there, I told him to swing
over to St. Charles and drop me at Louisiana instead.

I was working on pure intuition—maybe the closest
thing to principle I had. Connections were being made,
switches getting thrown, at some level not accessible to
me. I only had to go with it, ride it.

I went up those stairs and into the kitchen as though
it were my own. Heard the rasp and scuttle of someone
else in the next room.

I stepped in and saw Treadwell's kid bent over the
mattress in the niche. Late sunlight threw a perfect print
of miniblinds against one wall.

"Find what you're looking for?''

How often does it happen, after all?

He straightened. "Who the fuck are *you*?'' He came
up and around and had a gun in hand. The .38 from
under the chair cushion. I saw his eyes and knew what
was going to happen.

The choice was clear: stand still and get shot straight

on, or move and possibly, just possibly, minimize damage.

So instinctively I dove to the left. It felt as though someone had slammed the heel of his hand, hard, against my right shoulder. I was watching his face, then suddenly the back wall. Couldn't feel my right side at all. Then I was out for a while.

I came to on the stretcher. Saw my father's face upside down as they hoisted me into an ambulance. Lots of other faces watching.

"I've been wanting to talk to you," I told him.

"You're gonna be okay," he said. "It's not bad. Take some deep breaths."

"I miss you, Dad."

"We've stopped the bleeding. Try to be still. There's a needle in your hand, for fluids, just a precaution."

"You both were sitting on the car. You looked so young, so happy. What happened?"

"You've been shot, Mr. Griffin. You're going to be okay."

I caromed down a hall and into a room with bright lights overhead. An authoritative voice: the resident. Deferential ones: staff nurses. And one other.

"Mr. Griffin. Lewis. I know you can hear me. You're going to be all right. Listen to me."

A British accent. Wouldn't you know.

38

IT WAS GOOD THEATER, AS THEY SAY, MEANING THAT the playwright's contrived a way to get all his themes and characters and the underwear of his plot with its bad elastic crowded onstage at play's end for the big finale.

The old man lies on his sickbed and people file in and out, dragging behind them like bags of wool the very stuff of his life: his forfeitures and silences, his assumptions, his regrets.

So, propped up on pillows in my float of a bed with arm and shoulder taped firmly in place, for several days I held court, an improbable Rex, as faces streamed by: Walsh, Chip Landrieu, Richard Garces, Tito, Alouette.

Once, early on, I dreamed that Treadwell's son was there. Standing against a blue plaster wall, otherwise surrounded by sky, he held a gun loosely in hand. A flag had come out of the gun's barrel and unfurled; it read *Bang*. He said: You will not find me, get this sad certainty firmly in your head. Quoting Cocteau.

Another time LaVerne was there, eyes brimming with the world's pain and all the things left unsaid between us as she silently approached and leaned down to kiss me. Take care of my girl, she said. I awoke with a jolt of disorientation and loss.

Sometime on the third or fourth day, Walsh brought Treadwell by, as I'd asked, and I told him what I knew, sensing the spill of despair into his life. He kept his head down, thanked me and left. Walsh and I sat looking at one another a moment, then he shook his own head and followed.

Alouette was there when I first awoke, and came by the next two afternoons, after work. Things were fine at home, she told me, and she'd be starting school in January. Her father had called once or twice, but just to talk. And oh, yeah, before she forgot, a couple of things had come up at the house that she needed money for. I gave her most of what I had on me and said if she needed more, let me know.

But I *did* know, of course. Knew as surely as I think Dean Treadwell must have known. Even if, at the time, I declined putting it into words.

Alouette didn't show up the next day, and when I called the house, I got myself on the answering machine. I tried again two or three times that night, then again in the morning.

I was standing in front of a mirror, trying to figure out what to do with the other half of the shirt I'd managed to get my left arm into, when the doctor who operated on me came by on rounds. His name was Kowalski, he was chief resident on the surgical service, came from Chicago and was a rock climber. Most of our conversation had been about the last. Three years ago in Arizona a friend climbing beside him, another resident, had fallen and broken his back. Kowalski had immobilized him with climbing rope and sections he hollowed from saguaro cactus, lashed together a rough travois and carried him out. The friend had made a full recovery. Somehow you got the idea that nothing in the surgeon's formal practice was ever going to live up to that one bright segment of improvisation.

"Good. You're up," he said.

"Up. Yes, and going home."

"I'd have to recommend most urgently against that, Mr. Griffin."

"Recommend away." I turned to face him. "Look, I appreciate what you've done. And I'm more than willing to accede to whatever continuing treatment you prescribe. But the truth is, I don't have insurance, I can lie around at home every bit as well as I can here, and meanwhile there are things to be taken care of."

I suppose I should have said *truths are*.

"You'll promise to come in first thing in the morning?"

I nodded.

"Through ER. Just tell them I'm expecting you for a follow-up, and to beep me. It's against hospital policy, but they're used to it. I'll be here—somewhere. That way I can officially discharge you now and you won't have to go AMA, which can always lead to problems farther down the road."

"American Medical Association?"

"Against medical advice."

He helped drape the shirt and button it, then went out to the desk to do the paperwork. I joined him there eventually, shook hands and thanked him again.

"They're going to ask for a deposit downstairs at the business office. I'm sure they'll even insist that it's mandatory, but it isn't. The hospital's supported by public funds and legally they can't demand payment. Just tell them you don't have any money with you."

I didn't have. And as it turned out, they didn't ask, probably because I didn't go by the office.

I got a cab outside the hospital, had the driver take me home and wait while I went in to get money. Like most people who've been poor and on the streets, I had cash squirreled away in various spots around the house. Alouette had found some of the stashes, but others were intact. I took the driver a ten, doubling his fare, and came back in for the damage report.

Everything was still in her room except for clothes, personal items and a small suitcase. It seemed to me there were a few vacancies on the shelves, with books canting into them where others had been removed, but I couldn't be sure. Maybe I only wanted it to be so.

I found her note in the kitchen, on the table around

which, in the best southern tradition, we'd sat night after night talking.

> *Lewis,*
>
> *I think you're okay, your arm I mean, and I think by now you have to know something's wrong. You probably have a good idea what it is.*
>
> *I tried so hard, I really did. I hope you can give me credit for that. But everything's so* ordinary *now, so* plain.
>
> *I can't do this any longer. I don't want to hurt you, and I know that I will unless I go now. Of course, I'll hurt you either way, won't I? There's just not any way to win.*
>
> *It would be nice if I could believe I'm doing something good by leaving, but I guess that would only be fooling myself. And I don't need any more practice at that.*
>
> *Thank you for everything you did and tried to do for me, Lew. And thank you most of all for loving my mother. Yes, I remember that.*
>
> Alouette

39

YEARS WERE TO PASS BEFORE I SAW ALOUETTE AGAIN.

I rented a car that very afternoon, of course, and drove back up to Mississippi, scouting roadsides the whole way. I had midnight dinner with Sergeant Travis, left my suitcase for a few days at Dee's-Lux Inn but was mostly away from the room, spent two nights at a Quality Inn in Memphis. Then drove one-armed and empty-handed back to New Orleans. No sign of Alouette anywhere.

Mardi Gras is just over as I sit on a bright Ash Wednesday by the window in the upstairs front room writing this. All week I've looked down to watch crowds swarm toward St. Charles for parades, people stroll past at all hours in mask and costume, young women in pairs with backpacks and cotton sweaters, men with the plastic webbing of six-packs looped into their belts. Now the street is awash in trash: beer and soft-drink cans, waxed paper cups, containers from Popeye's and Taco Bell, discarded strings of beads, broken doubloons. The old house creaks around me. A tree limb screeches at the pane, and from somewhere behind, deep within the house, a dull moan starts up each time the wind peaks.

Some inchoate equation between the masking and forced revelry of Mardi Gras, the expert self-deception Alouette recognized in herself, and my own in this account, suggests itself. Finally there's little enough difference between them.

I remember that Robbe-Grillet, at work on *Le Voyeur*, traveled briefly to the Brittany coast to refresh his memory of its setting and found that he had no interest in actual gulls, that he cared now only for the gulls of his fiction.

This much is true: Alouette was gone. And I was left thinking, in that self-engaged manner we all have when suddenly alone, that it all had been for nothing.

But maybe (I thought then) something would come of it after all. Maybe we do good things, things that matter, without ever realizing it. Maybe those are the best things we do.

Or maybe, just as Alouette tried so hard to believe her departure might be virtuous, that is just something I want to believe. We betray ourselves into going on; but it's also given us to choose the form of that betrayal.

Alouette was gone. Gone into the darkness that took my son, the darkness that took her mother, the darkness that is so much in us all.

I sat looking for a long time out into that darkness. It was almost midnight, with a chance of rain. The phone's ringing brought me around. I answered.

"Lew," and when she took time getting the next word out, I knew it was Clare. "How are you? I just heard, a few minutes ago. About Alouette."

"It's not like it's wholly unexpected."

"That does nothing to diminish the pain."

"No," I said. "It doesn't. Except maybe in movies about boys learning to be men."

"Pain can be good, Lew. The same as other strong feelings. Love, fear, devotion. It can give us reasons to go on when there aren't any others. It can become a new center for a new self."

Or an excuse for all sorts of evasions.

But I said: "You're proof of that, Clare."

"Of course, it can also give us a reason to make a perfect fool of ourself at eleven o'clock at night."

"Is that what you're doing?"

"God. I hope not." She was silent for a few moments. "I guess what I'm doing, really, is using the situation as an excuse to call and say how much I miss you. Yeah. I'm pretty sure that's it.''

"I miss you too. More than you can know."

"You could have called."

"No, Clare. I couldn't."

"Okay. So I never was much good at these coy, girlish ploys. Give me credit for trying. I was supposed to call *you*. And now I'm doing that."

"It's good to hear your voice," I said after a moment.

"I'd like to see you, Lew."

A moth fluttered into my window's light again and again.

"Okay."

"If that's all right with you."

"It is."

"You understand . . ."

"I think so. I'd like to see you, whatever I do or don't understand."

"Maybe we could have a drink."

"That would be great. Where?"

"I don't know. Tip's, maybe?"

"*Ça va.*"

"Want me to pick you up?"

"I've had enough car for a while. I'll walk. See you there. Give me fifteen, twenty minutes."

"Oh, Lew, I almost forgot: Bat came home. I went out Tuesday morning and there he was, sitting on the car, like nothing ever happened."

"Nearest thing he could find to his fridge, I guess."

"I guess. God, I'm looking forward to seeing you."

"Then go saddle up your car, scrape off any stray nesting cats and drive if you'll excuse the expression like a—"

"Don't say it!"

"—good friend."

"I hope so, Lew. I do so want to be."

"See you soon. Calm seas, Clare."

And I walked out into the darkness toward her.

Four streets up, hearing voices close by as I came to a corner, I turned my head. Further down the block, a mugging was taking place. It had begun that way, at least; now it seemed to be progressing. One of the men had the woman's purse over his own shoulder. He knelt at her head, holding her down with hands flat against her shoulders and licking upside down at her face while the other one's hands burrowed roughly under her skirt. As I watched, that one reached up and slapped her hard on the cheek, then took her neck in his hand.

I shouted and started toward them, instinctively turning to keep the injured arm out of sight. Both jumped to their feet. The one who had been at her head ran. The other stood his ground till I came closer and slipped my hand into my coat pocket. Then he also bolted.

"Are you all right?" I asked. A plain woman in her early thirties, inexpensively dressed.

"I think so."

"Don't be afraid," I told her.

Then I, too, was running.

SENSATIONAL
87TH PRECINCT NOVELS
FROM THE GRAND MASTER

ED McBAIN

KISS	71382-9/$5.99 US/$6.99 Can
LULLABY	70384-X/$5.99 US/$6.99 Can
POISON	70030-1/$4.99 US/$5.99 Can
EIGHT BLACK HORSES	70029-8/$4.99 US/$5.99 Can
LIGHTNING	69974-5/$4.95 US/$5.95 Can
ICE	67108-5/$5.99 US/$6.99 Can
VESPERS	70385-8/$5.99 US/$7.99 Can
WIDOWS	71383-7/$5.99 US/$6.99 Can
CALYPSO	70591-5/$4.99 US/$6.99 Can
DOLL	70082-4/$4.50 US/$5.50 Can
LONG TIME NO SEE	70369-6/$4.99 US/$5.99 Can
MISCHIEF	71384-5/$5.99 US/$6.99 Can